# At The Back of the North Wind

George MacDonald

BETHANY HOUSE PUBLISHERS
MINNEAPOLIS, MINNESOTA 55438

A specially edited version of George MacDonald's classic *At the Back of the North Wind*, by Michael R. Phillips.

Illustrations reprinted by permission of Macmillan Publishing company from *At the Back of the North Wind* by George MacDonald, illustrated by F.D. Bedford. Copyright © 1924 Macmillan Publishing Company.

Cover illustration by Dan Thornberg,
Bethany House Publishers staff artist.



Published by Bethany House Publishers
A Ministry of Bethany Fellowship, Inc.
6820 Auto Club Road, Minneapolis, Minnesota 55438

Printed in the United States of America

**Library of Congress Cataloging-in-Publication Data**

MacDonald, George, 1824–1905.
At the back of the North Wind / George MacDonald ; edited by Michael R. Phillips.
p. cm.
Summary: Diamond, a young boy living in nineteenth-century London, has many adventures as he travels with the beautiful Lady North Wind and comes to know the many facets of her personality.

[1. Fairy tales.] I. Phillips. Michael R. , 1946– . II. Title.
PZ8.M1754At 1991
[Fic]—dc20 90–23483
CIP
ISBN 1–55661–196–X AC

**BETHANY HOUSE PUBLISHERS**
Minneapolis, Minnesota 55438

**The Novels of George MacDonald Edited for Today's Reader**

| **Edited Title** | **Original Title** |
|---|---|
| *The Fisherman's Lady* | *Malcolm* |
| *The Marquis' Secret* | *The Marquis of Lossie* |
| *The Baronet's Song* | *Sir Gibbie* |
| *The Shepherd's Castle* | *Donal Grant* |
| *The Tutor's First Love* | *David Elginbrod* |
| *The Musician's Quest* | *Robert Falconer* |
| *The Maiden's Bequest* | *Alec Forbes* |
| *The Curate's Awakening* | *Thomas Wingfold* |
| *The Lady's Confession* | *Paul Faber* |
| *The Baron's Apprenticeship* | *There and Back* |
| *The Highlander's Last Song* | *What's Mine's Mine* |
| *The Gentlewoman's Choice* | *Weighed and Wanting* |
| *The Laird's Inheritance* | *Warlock O'Glenwarlock* |
| *The Minister's Restoration* | *Salted with Fire* |
| *A Daughter's Devotion* | *Mary Marston* |
| *The Peasant Girl's Dream* | *Heather and Snow* |
| *The Landlady's Master* | *The Elect Lady* |
| *The Poet's Homecoming* | *Home Again* |

**MacDonald Classics Edited for Young Readers**

*Wee Sir Gibbie of the Highlands*
*Alec Forbes and His Friend Annie*
*At the Back of the North Wind*

---

*George MacDonald: Scotland's Beloved Storyteller* by Michael Phillips
*Discovering the Character of God* by George MacDonald
*Knowing the Heart of God* by George MacDonald

# Sunrise Books, Publishers

Eureka, California 95501

**The Sunrise Centenary Editions of the Original Works of George MacDonald in Leatherbound Collector's Editions**

**Novels**

Alec Forbes of Howglen
Sir Gibbie
Thomas Wingfold, Curate
Malcolm
Salted with Fire
The Elect Lady

**Sermons**

Unspoken Sermons I
The Hope of the Gospel

**Poems**

A Hidden Life & Other Poems
The Disciple and Other Poems

**The Masterline Series of Studies and Essays About George MacDonald**

*From a Northern Window: A Personal Remembrance of George MacDonald* by his son Ronald MacDonald

*The Harmony Within: The Spiritual Vision of George MacDonald* by Rolland Hein

*George MacDonald's Fiction: A Twentieth-Century View* by Richard Reis

*God's Fiction: Symbolism and Allegory in the Works of George MacDonald* by David Robb

MICHAEL PHILLIPS, who lives in Eureka, California, has always loved books. He writes books and sells books (he operates a bookstore on the West Coast) and always wants to share his favorites with others. When he discovered George MacDonald nearly twenty years ago, one of his great ambitions became to reacquaint the public (both children and adults) with the writings and stories of this Scottish author of the nineteenth century. He has edited many of MacDonald's novels for grown-ups, and some of his edited editions have become bestsellers. *At the Back of the North Wind* is part of a new series of MacDonald books written for young readers.

# Contents

# Introduction

George MacDonald was a Scottish writer who lived in the last century (1824–1905) and wrote more than fifty books. He was a good friend of many famous authors such as Charles Dickens, Mark Twain, and Lewis Carroll (who wrote *Alice in Wonderland)* but is not as well known now as some of his friends.

One of the things George MacDonald loved doing more than anything else was telling stories to children. He had eleven sons and daughters of his own and enjoyed making up stories for them. He wrote over a dozen books for children, and many more short stories, in addition to the thirty or forty books he authored for adults.

George MacDonald came from a farming family who lived in the north of Scotland. All of his life he was extremely fond of horses, and it may have been in his own father's stables that the first ideas for this book came to him.

When he grew up, George MacDonald wrote a story about a little boy who liked to listen to the wind through the walls of his own hayloft. In fact, this story (which was first published in 1871) became MacDonald's most popular book of all, and is still, more than a hundred years later, many people's favorite MacDonald book. When George MacDonald first wrote *At the Back of the North Wind,* it was very long and some parts were a little hard to understand. People at that time talked differently than we do today, and books sounded different too. But since I enjoyed this story so much and wanted to share it with you, I thought I could shorten it a little and make the language easier for you to understand. That way you will be able to read and enjoy *At the Back of the North Wind* for yourself.

I hope you enjoy little Diamond's adventures with his friend North Wind. And I hope George MacDonald becomes your friend as he has mine, and that you will want to read more of his books after you have finished with this one.

Michael Phillips

# Chapter One

# Diamond Meets the North Wind

I have been asked to tell you about the back of the north wind. So I am going to relate a story about a boy who went there.

Little Diamond lived with his parents in a low room over a coach house. One side of it was built only of boards, and the boards were so old that you might stick a small knife through them into the outside. But even so, this room was not terribly cold, except when the north wind blew stronger than usual.

But the room where Diamond slept was always cold, except in summer. Indeed, I am not sure whether I ought to call it a room at all, for it was just a loft where they kept hay and straw and oats for the horses. Diamond's father was a coachman for a wealthy businessman by the name of Mr. Coleman, who lived in London. The father had named the boy after a favorite horse. Because they had so little room in their own end over the place where the coaches were kept, Diamond's father had built him a bed in the loft over the horses. And Diamond's father put old Diamond in the stall below, right underneath where the boy's bed stood, because the horse was quiet and did not go to sleep standing but lay down like other creatures.

There was hay at the boy's feet and hay at his head, piled up to the very roof. The stock of hay was always gradually being used up for the horses, until those times when it would suddenly be replenished. Sometimes, when the hay was nearly gone, the whole space of the loft, with the little windowpanes in the roof for the stars to look in, would lie empty and open before the boy's eyes as he lay in bed. At other times, after a new supply had just been added, a yellow wall of sweet-smelling grasses closed up his view of the sky.

Sometimes when his mother had undressed him in her room and told him to trot to bed by himself, he would creep into the heart of the pile of hay and lie there thinking how cold it was outside in the wind, and how warm it would be inside his bed, and how he could go to it whenever he wanted. Only he wouldn't just yet. He would get a little colder first. At last he would scramble out of the hay, shoot like an arrow into his bed, cover himself up, and snuggle down, thinking what a happy boy he was. He had not the least idea that the wind got in at a chink in the wall and blew about him all night. For the back of his bed was made of thin boards only an inch thick. And on the other side of them was the north wind.

One night after he lay down, little Diamond found that a knot had come out of one of the crumbly boards of the wall. He didn't like to leave things wrong; so he jumped out of bed, got a little piece of hay, twisted it up, folded it in the middle, and stuck it into the hole in the wall.

But the wind began to blow louder, and just as Diamond was beginning to fall asleep, out blew his little hay-cork and hit him on the nose. He got up, searched for his piece of hay, found it, stuck it in harder, and was just dropping off once more when, pop! the cork struck him again, this time on the cheek. Up he rose again, made a fresh twist of hay, and corked the hole as hard as he could. But he had hardly lain down again before—pop! it landed on his forehead. He gave up, drew the covers above his head, and was soon fast asleep.

The next day Diamond forgot all about the hole by his bed. His mother, however, discovered it, and pasted a bit of brown paper over it. When Diamond snuggled down the next night, he did not even think about it.

Presently, however, he lifted his head and listened.

Who could that be talking to him? The wind was rising again and getting very loud and full of rushes and whistles. Diamond sat up and listened. The voice seemed to come from the back of his head. He crept nearer to the sound and laid his ear against the wall. But he heard nothing but the wind, which sounded very loud indeed. But the moment he moved his head away from the wall, he heard the voice again, close to his ear. He felt about and his hand came upon the piece of paper his mother had pasted over the hole. He laid his ear against it again and then he heard the voice quite clearly. There was a little corner of the paper loose, and through that, as from a mouth in the wall, the voice was coming.

"What do you mean, little boy—closing up my window?"

"What window?" asked Diamond.

"You stuffed hay into it three times last night. I had to blow it out again three times."

"You can't mean this little hole," replied Diamond. "It isn't a window. It's just a hole in the wall by my bed."

"I did not say it was *a* window I said it was *my* window."

"But it can't be a window. Windows are holes to see out of," said Diamond.

"But that's just what I want this window for."

"But you are outside. You can't need a window."

"You are mistaken, little boy. As you say, windows are to see out of. Well, I'm in my house out here, and I want windows to see out of it."

"But you've made a window into my bed."

"Well, your mother has three windows into my dancing room, and you have three into my attic right above your head."

"You must have a tall house then," said Diamond.

"Yes, a very tall house. The whole sky is my house. The clouds are inside it."

"Dear me," said Diamond, and thought a minute. "I think, then, that you can hardly expect me to keep a window in my bed for you. Why don't you make a window into someone else's bed? So many people have much nicer beds for you to look at than mine."

"It's not the bed I care about. It's what's in it. But you just open that window."

"Well, Mother says I should be agreeable. But I really don't want to open it. You see, if I do, the north wind will blow right in my face."

"I am the north wind."

"Oh-o-oh!" said Diamond thoughtfully. "Then will you promise not to blow on my face if I open your window?"

"I can't promise that."

"But you'll give me a toothache. Mother's got it already."

"But what's to become of me without a window?"

"I'm sure I don't know. All I can say is it will be worse for me than for you."

"No, it will not. I promise you that. You will be much the better for it. Just you believe what I say and do as I tell you."

"Well, I *can* pull the blankets over my head if it gets too cold," replied Diamond. He reached out and felt in the dark with his little sharp fingernails, got hold of the loose edge of the paper, and tore it off.

In came a long, whistling spear of cold and struck his naked little chest. He scrambled under his blankets and covered himself up. Now there was no paper between him and the voice and he felt a little frightened. What a strange person this North Wind must be that lived in the great house called out-of-doors and who made doors into people's beds!

But the voice began again, and he could hear it quite plainly, even with his head under the blankets. It was a more gentle voice now, although six times as large and loud as it had been, and he thought it sounded a little like his mother's.

"What is your name, little boy?" it asked.

"Diamond," answered Diamond, under the covers.

"Do you know to whom you are speaking?"

"No," said Diamond, for to know a person's name is not always to know the person's self.

"Do you know what a diamond is?"

"Of course. Diamond is very nice, and so quiet all night. Until the morning when he gets up on his four huge legs. It's like thunder!"

"You don't seem to know what a diamond is."

"Oh, don't I! Diamond is a great big horse, and he sleeps right under me. He is old Diamond and I am young Diamond. Or if you like it better, for you're very particular, Mr. North Wind, he's big Diamond and I'm little Diamond. And I don't know which of us my father likes best."

A beautiful laugh, large but very soft and musical, sounded somewhere beside him, but Diamond kept his head under the covers.

"I'm not Mr. North Wind," said the voice.

"You told me that you were the north wind," insisted Diamond.

"I did not say *Mister* North Wind," said the voice.

"Well, I added the Mister because Mother says I ought to be polite."

"It doesn't seem polite to lie there talking with your head under the bedclothes without ever looking up to see what kind of person you are talking to. I want you to come out with me."

"I want to go to sleep," said Diamond, very nearly crying, for he did not like to be scolded, even when he deserved it.

"You shall sleep all the better tomorrow night. Now, will you take your head out from under the covers?" said the voice.

"No," answered Diamond, half annoyed, half frightened.

The instant he said the word a tremendous blast of wind crashed in a board of the wall and swept the covers off Diamond. He jumped up in terror. Leaning over him was the large, beautiful, pale face of a woman. Her dark flashing eyes looked a little angry. But a quivering in her upper lip made her look as if she were going to cry. Away from her head streamed black hair in every direction, so that the darkness in the hayloft looked as if it were made of her hair.

Diamond gazed at her in speechless amazement, entranced with her beauty. Her hair then began to gather itself out of the darkness and fall down all about her again till her face looked out of the midst of it like a moon out of a cloud. From her eyes came all the light by which Diamond could see her. The wind died down and in a moment it was completely still.

"I am sorry I was forced to be so rough with you. Will you

go with me now, you little Diamond?" asked the lady.

"I will. Yes, I will," answered Diamond, holding out both his arms. "But," he added, dropping them, "how shall I get my clothes? They are in Mother's room."

"Oh, never mind your clothes. You will not be cold. I shall take care of that. Nobody is cold with the north wind."

"I thought everybody was cold because of the north wind," said Diamond.

"That is a great mistake. Most people are cold because they are *not* with the north wind, but away from it."

If Diamond had been a little older and had supposed himself a good deal wiser, he would have thought the lady was joking. But he was not older, and he did not fancy himself wiser, and therefore understood her well enough. Again he stretched out his arms.

"Follow me, Diamond," she said.

"Yes," said Diamond.

"You're not afraid?" asked the North Wind.

"No, ma'am. But Mother would never let me go out without shoes. She never says anything about clothes, so I daresay she wouldn't mind that."

"I know your mother very well," said the lady. "She is a good woman. I have visited her often. I was with her when you were born. I saw her laugh and cry, both at once. I love your mother, Diamond."

"How was it you did not know my name, then, ma'am? Please, am I to say *ma'am* to you, ma'am?"

"One question at a time, dear boy. I knew your name quite well, but I wanted to hear what you would say for it. Your name is in the Bible—the sixth stone in the high priest's breastplate."

"Oh!—a stone, was it?" said Diamond. "I thought it had been a horse—I did."

"Never mind. A horse is better than a stone any day. Well, you see, I know all about you and your mother. Now for the next question. You're not to call me *ma'am*. You must call me just by my own name—respectfully, you know—just North Wind."

"Well, please, North Wind, you are so beautiful, I am quite ready to go with you."

"You must not be ready to go with everything beautiful, Diamond."

"But what's beautiful can't be bad. You're not bad, North Wind?"

"No, I'm not bad. But sometimes beautiful things grow bad by doing bad, and it takes some time for their badness to spoil their beauty. So little boys may be mistaken if they go after things just because they are beautiful."

"Well, I will go with you because you are beautiful and good too."

"Ah, but there's another thing, Diamond. What if I should suddenly look ugly, but still not be bad—look ugly myself because I am making ugly things beautiful? What then?"

"I don't quite understand you, North Wind."

"I will tell you, then. If you see my face become all black, don't be frightened. If you see me flapping wings like a bat's, as big as the whole sky, don't be frightened. Or even if you see me looking in at people's windows or raging ten times worse than Mrs. Bill, the blacksmith's wife—you must believe that I am doing my work. And, Diamond, even if I change into a snake or a tiger, you must not let go your hold of me, for my hand will never change in yours if you keep a good hold. If you keep a hold, you will know who I am all the time, even when you look at me and I don't look the least like the north wind. Even if I look like something awful. Do you understand?"

"Quite well," replied little Diamond.

"Come along then," said North Wind, and she disappeared behind the mountain of hay.

Diamond crept out of bed and followed her.

## Chapter Two

# In the Yard

When Diamond got around the corner of the hay he hesitated. The stairway down to the door was at the other end of the loft, and it looked very black indeed, for it was full of North Wind's hair as she descended in front of him. But right beside him was the ladder going straight down into the stable. His father always came up it to fetch the hay for the horses' dinner. And through the opening in the floor the faint gleam of the stable lantern was inviting. It looked so much nicer than that black stairway. So Diamond thought he would go down that way instead.

When Diamond the boy was halfway down, he remembered that the stable door would be locked, so it would be no use to go down this way. But at the same moment horse Diamond's great head poked out of his stall and looked toward the ladder. He knew boy Diamond very well and wanted him to pull old Diamond's ears for him. This, Diamond did very gently for a minute or so, and stroked his neck too, and kissed the big horse, and was taking bits of straw and hay out of his mane when all at once he remembered that the lady North Wind was waiting for him in the yard.

"Good night, Diamond," he said, and darted back up the

ladder, across the loft, and down the dark stairway to the door. But when he got out into the yard, there was no lady to be seen.

Now it is always a dreadful thing to think there is somebody there, and find nobody. And Diamond was especially disappointed, for his little heart had been beating with joy: the face of North Wind was so grand! To have a lady like that for a friend—with such long hair, too! Why, it was longer than twenty Diamonds' tails!

But she was gone. And there he stood, with his bare feet on the stones of the paved yard.

It was a clear night overhead and the stars were shining. But the moon was only a poor thin crescent. There was just one great jagged black and gray cloud in the sky. Diamond had never been out so late in all his life, and everything looked so strange about him!—just as if he had gotten into Fairyland. And if you had been out in the face and not at the back of the north wind, on a rather cold and frosty night, and just in your nightgown, you would have felt it all quite as strange as Diamond did. He cried a little, for he was so disappointed to lose the lady. But I don't mind people crying so much as I mind what they cry about, and how they cry—whether they cry like ladies and gentlemen, or go shrieking about full of anger and bad temper.

But it can't be denied that a little gentle crying does one good. It did Diamond good, for as soon as it was over he was a brave boy again.

"She must be hiding somewhere to see what I will do," decided Diamond. "I will look for her."

So he went round the end of the stable toward the kitchen. But the moment he was past the shelter of the stable wall, the wind came sharp as a knife against his little chest and bare legs. He went on to look in the garden, but there the wind was blowing even stronger till he could hardly fight against it. And it was so cold!

Then he remembered what the lady had said about people being cold because they were not *with* the north wind. All at once he seemed to understand what she meant. If she had told him that he must hold his face to the wind, Diamond would have done it. But right now he thought Lady North Wind had said something like telling him to get *with* her. So he turned his back to the wind and trotted back toward the yard. And strange to say, it blew so much more gently against the back of his calves that he hardly felt it. It was just as if the wind were pushing him along. If he turned around, it grew very sharp on his legs, and so he thought the wind might really be Lady North Wind, though he could not see her, and he had better let her blow him wherever she pleased.

So she blew and blew, and he went and went, until he found himself standing in the middle of the lawn in front of Mr. Coleman's house. Mr. Coleman was his father's master and the owner of Diamond and the coaches and the stable where they lived. The soft grass felt good to his bare feet, and almost warm after the stones of the yard. But the lady was nowhere to be seen. Then he began to wonder if she was offended with him for not following close behind her but staying to talk to the horse.

There he stood in the middle of the lawn, the wind blowing his nightgown till it flapped like a loose sail. Diamond stood all alone in the strange night and began to wonder whether he was in a dream or not. *It is important to determine this; for,* thought Diamond, *if I am in a dream, I am safe in my bed, and I don't need to cry. But if I'm not in a dream, I'm out here, and perhaps I had better cry, or at least I'm not sure if I can help it.* Finally he came to the conclusion that whether he was in a dream or not, there could be no harm in not crying for a little while longer. He could always begin whenever he liked.

The back of Mr. Coleman's house faced the lawn, and the light was still shining in one of the windows. The ladies had not yet gone to bed, but they had no idea that a little boy was standing out on the lawn in his nightgown. As long as he saw that light, Diamond could not feel quite so lonely. He had been in that room once or twice that he could remember at Christmastimes. For the Colemans were kind people, though they did not care much about children.

All at once the light went out. Then, indeed, he felt that he was left alone. It was dreadful to be out in the night after *everybody* had gone to bed! That was more than he could bear. He burst out crying with a wail.

Perhaps you think this was foolish of him, for couldn't he just go home to his bed whenever he liked?

Yes, but it seemed so dreadful to him to creep up that dark stairway again and lie down in his bed, all the time knowing that North Wind's window was open beside him, and she was gone and he might never see her again. He would be just as lonely there as here.

At the very moment when he burst out crying, the old nurse who had grown to be one of the family came to the back door to close the shutters. She thought she heard a cry, put a hand on each side of her eyes, peered through the glass, and thought she saw something white on the lawn. Too old and too wise to be frightened, she opened the door and went straight toward the white thing to see what it was. And when Diamond saw her coming he was not frightened either, though Mrs. Crump was a little cross sometimes—but she was a good kind of cross. So she came up with her neck stretched out, peering into the night to see what it could be glimmering white in front of her. When she did see, she made a great exclamation and threw up her hands. Then without a word, for she thought Diamond was walking in his sleep, she took hold of him and led him toward the house. He made no objection and walked straight inside with her.

Miss Coleman was sitting brushing her hair in the drawing room because the fire in her bedroom had gone out. The young lady was very lovely, though not nearly so beautiful as North Wind, and her hair was extremely long—though nothing at all like North Wind's hair. Yet when she looked around, with her hair all about her, as Diamond entered, he thought for one moment that it was North Wind. He pulled his hand from Mrs. Crump's and ran toward Miss Coleman with his arms outstretched. She was so pleased that she put down her brush and half knelt on the floor, ready to receive him in her arms.

He saw the next moment that she was not Lady North Wind, but she looked so much like her that he could not help running into her arms and crying all over again. Mrs. Crump said the poor child had walked out in his sleep, and for anything Diamond knew, maybe it was true. He let them talk on about him and said nothing.

After their surprise was over, Miss Coleman gave him a piece of sponge cake, and Mrs. Crump took him to his mother.

When Mrs. Crump knocked, his mother had to get out of bed to open the door. She was indeed surprised to see her boy. She took him in her arms and carried him to his bed, and then returned to have a long talk with Mrs. Crump. They were still talking when Diamond fell fast asleep, and then he could hear them no longer.

CHAPTER
THREE

# ANOTHER VISIT

Diamond woke very early the next morning. His first thought was about the curious dream he had the night before. But the memory grew brighter and brighter until it no longer seemed like a dream at all, and he began to think that maybe he really had been out in the wind last night. He came to the conclusion that if Mrs. Crump really had brought him home, his mother would say something to him about it, and that would settle the matter. Then he got up and dressed himself, but finding that his father and mother were still in bed he went down the ladder to the stable. There he found that even old Diamond was not awake yet and was lying as flat as a horse could lie on his nice clean bed of straw.

*I'll give old Diamond a surprise,* thought the boy. He crept up very softly, and before the horse knew little Diamond was there he got astride his friend's back. But then it was Diamond's turn to be surprised. For just as suddenly as an earthquake, with a great rumbling and rocking and sprawling of legs and heaving of a horsey back, young Diamond found himself hoisted up in the air, and he hung on tight with both hands twisted in the horse's mane. He gave a cry of terror, but as soon as old Diamond heard young Diamond's cry, the horse knew there was nothing to kick about and then he stood still. For young Diamond was a good boy, and old Diamond was a good horse, and the one was all right on the back of the other.

As soon as Diamond had gotten himself comfortable on the saddle place, the horse began pulling at his hay and the boy began thinking. He had never mounted Diamond alone before, and he had never gotten off him without being lifted down. So he sat, while the horse ate, wondering how he was going to get back down to the ground.

But while he was thinking, his mother woke and her first thought was to see her boy. She had visited him twice during the night and found him sleeping quietly. Now his bed was empty, and she was frightened.

"Diamond! Diamond! Where are you, Diamond?" she called out.

Diamond turned his head where he sat like a knight on his steed, and cried aloud, "Here, Mother!"

"Where, Diamond?" she returned.

"Here, Mother, on Diamond's back."

She came running to the ladder, looked down, and saw him on top of the huge horse.

"Come down, Diamond," she said.

"I can't," answered Diamond.

"How did you get up?" asked his mother.

"Quite easily," he answered. "But when I got on top of him, Diamond stood up, and so here I am."

His mother thought he had been walking in his sleep again and hurried down the ladder. She did not much want to go up to the horse, for she had not been used to horses. But she would have gone into a lion's den, not to say a horse's stall, to help her boy. So she went and lifted him off Diamond's back and felt braver all her life after that. She carried him up to her room, but she said nothing about the previous night, for she did not want to frighten him at what she thought had been his own sleep-walking. Before the next day was over, Diamond had almost concluded that the whole adventure was a dream.

For a week his mother watched him very carefully. She went into the loft several times a night—as often as she woke. Every time she found him sound asleep.

All week the weather was cold. The grass was white in the morning from the frost which clung to every blade. And since Diamond's shoes were not very good, and his mother had not quite saved up enough money to get him the new pair she wanted for him, she would not let him go outside. He played all his games over and over indoors. He especially liked to drive two chairs harnessed to the baby's cradle. And if they did not go very fast, they went as fast as could be expected of the best chairs in the world, although one of them had only three legs and the other only half a back.

At length one day his mother brought home his new shoes, and no sooner did she find they fit him than she said he might run out in the yard for an hour.

The sun was going down when he ran through the door like a bird escaping from its cage. All the world was new to him again. A great fire of sunset burned on the top of the gate that led from the stables to the house. Above the fire in the sky lay a large lake of green light, above that a golden cloud, and over that the blue of the wintry heavens. And Diamond thought that, next to his own home, he had never seen any place he would like so much to live in as that sky. For it is not fine things that make a home a nice place, but your mother and your father.

As he was looking at the lovely colors, the gates were thrown open and there was old Diamond and his friend pulling the carriage, dancing with impatience to get back to their stalls and their oats. Into the yard they came. Diamond was not the least afraid of his father driving over him with the coach. But he did not want to spoil the grand show of the horses and the carriage and his father with his black and red cape, so he slipped out of the way so they could drive right through to the stables.

As he stood there he remembered how the wind had driven him about this same spot on the night of his dream. And once more he was almost sure it was no dream. Whether it was or not, he decided to go into the garden to see if things looked at all now as they did that night. He opened the door and went through the little belt of shrubbery. But not a flower was to be seen. Even the brave old chrysanthemums and roses were gone because of the frost. What? Yes! There was one! He ran and knelt down to look at it.

It was a primrose—small but perfectly shaped. As he stooped his face to see the flower up close, a little wind began to blow, and two or three long leaves that stood up behind the blossom shook and waved. But the primrose lay still in the green hollow, looking up at the sky and not seeming to know that the wind was blowing at all. It was just like one tiny eye that the wintry earth had opened to look at the sky with. All at once Diamond thought it was saying its prayers, and he ought not to be staring at it. So he jumped up and ran to the stable to see his father make Diamond's bed. Then his father picked him up in his arms, carried him up the ladder, and set him down at the table where they were going to have their supper.

"Miss is very poorly," said Diamond's father. "Mis'ess has been to the doctor with her today and she looked very glum when she came out again. I was watching them to see what the doctor had said."

"And did Miss look sad too?" asked his mother.

"Not half as sad as Mis'ess," returned the coachman. "You see—"

But he lowered his voice, and Diamond could not make out more than a word here and there. For Diamond's father was not only one of the finest coachmen and best drivers, but one of the most discreet of servants as well. Therefore he did not talk about the affairs of the Coleman family to anyone but his wife, and was careful that even Diamond should hear nothing he could repeat again concerning the master and his family.

It was bedtime soon and Diamond went to bed and fell sound asleep. He woke all at once, in the dark.

"Open the window, Diamond," said a voice.

Now, Diamond's mother had again pasted up North Wind's window.

"Are you North Wind?" asked Diamond. "I don't hear you blowing."

"No. But you hear me talking. Open the window, for I haven't much time."

"Yes," returned Diamond. "But please, North Wind, why? You left me all alone last time."

He had gotten up on his knees and was busy with his fingernails once more, trying to tear off the paper over the hole in the wall. For now that North Wind spoke to him again, he remembered all that had taken place before as clearly as if it had happened only last night.

"Yes, but that was your fault," returned North Wind. "I had work to do. And besides, a gentleman should never keep a lady waiting."

"But I'm not a gentleman," said Diamond, scratching away at the paper.

"I hope you won't say that ten years from now."

"I'm going to be a coachman, and a coachman is not a gentleman. Gentlemen are rich like Mr. Coleman."

"We call your father a gentleman in our house," said North Wind.

"He doesn't call himself one," replied Diamond.

"That doesn't matter. Every man ought to be a gentleman, whether he is rich or poor. And your father is one."

Diamond was so pleased to hear this that he scratched at the paper all the harder, and got hold of the edge of it and tore it off. The next instant a young girl glided across the bed and stood on the floor.

"Oh dear!" exclaimed Diamond, quite frightened. "I didn't know you were there. Who are you?"

"I'm North Wind."

"Are you really?"

"Yes. Now hurry."

"But you're no bigger than I am."

"Do you think I care about how big or little I am? Didn't you see me this evening? I was even smaller then."

"No. Where were you?"

"Behind the leaves of the primrose. Didn't you see them blowing?"

"Yes."

"Hurry, then, if you want to go with me."

"But you are not big enough to take care of me. I think you must be only *Miss* North Wind."

"I am big enough to show you the way at least. But if you

won't come with me, then you must stay behind."

"I have to get dressed first. I didn't mind with a grown lady, but I couldn't go with a little girl in my nightgown."

"Very well. I'm not in such a hurry as I was the other night. Dress as fast as you can and I'll go and shake the primrose leaves till you come."

"Don't hurt it," said Diamond.

North Wind broke out in a little laugh like the breaking of silver bubbles, and was gone in a moment. Diamond jumped out of bed and dressed himself as fast as he could. Then he crept out into the yard and to the primrose. Behind it stood North Wind, leaning over it and looking at the flower as if she had been its mother.

"Come along," she said, jumping up and holding out her hand.

Diamond took her hand. It was cold, but so pleasant and full of life, it was better than a warm one. She led him across the garden. With one bound she was suddenly on the top of the wall and Diamond was left down on the ground.

"Stop, stop!" he cried. "Please, I can't jump like that."

North Wind reached down and Diamond took hold of her hand again, gave a great jump, and the next instant was standing beside her.

"This *is* nice," he said.

They made one more jump and stood in the road by the river. The river was full, for it was high tide. And the stars were shining clear in its depths. The water lay still, waiting for the bend in its course where it ran into the sea. They walked along its side. But they had not walked far before its surface was covered with ripples and the reflection of the stars had vanished.

North Wind was now tall as a full-grown girl. Her hair was flying about her head and the wind was blowing a breeze down the river. But she turned aside and went up a narrow street, and as she walked her hair fell down around her and the breeze stopped.

"I have some rather disagreeable work to do tonight," she said, "before I go out to sea. And I must begin at once."

Then she took hold of Diamond's hand and began to run,

gliding faster and faster. Diamond kept up with her as well as he could. She made many turnings and windings. Once they ran through a hall where they found both the back and front door open. At the foot of the stair North Wind stopped and stood still, and hearing a great growl, Diamond jumped back in terror. There, instead of North Wind, was a huge wolf by his side. He let go his hold and the wolf bounded up the stair. The windows of the house rattled and shook as if guns were firing and there was a sound of something falling from above him. Diamond stood staring up at the landing with his face white with fear.

Coming to himself all at once, he rushed after her with his little fist clenched. There were ladies in long dresses going up and down the stairs, and gentlemen in white neckties who stared at him, but none of them said anything. Before he reached the top of the stair, however, North Wind met him, took him by the hand, and hurried him out of the house.

"I hope you haven't eaten a baby, North Wind!" said Diamond.

North Wind laughed merrily and went tripping on even faster. Her grassy robe swept and swirled about her steps, and wherever it passed over withered leaves, they went whirling in spirals all about her feet.

"No," she said at last, "I did not eat a baby. You would not have asked that foolish question if you had not let go of my hand. You would have seen how I took care of a nurse who was calling a child bad names and telling her she was wicked. She had been drinking. I saw an ugly gin bottle in a cupboard."

"And you frightened her?" said Diamond.

"I believe so," answered North Wind, laughing merrily. "I jumped at her throat and she tumbled over on the floor with such a crash that they ran in. She'll be fired tomorrow—and just in time, if they knew as much as I do."

"But didn't you frighten the baby?"

"She never saw me. The woman would not have seen me either if she had not been wicked."

"Oh," said Diamond, with a questioning look.

"Why should you be able to see things," returned North Wind, "that you wouldn't understand? Good people see good things; bad people, bad things."

"Then you are a bad thing?"

"No. For *you* see me, Diamond, dear," said North Wind, looking down at him, and Diamond saw the loving eyes of the great lady beaming from the depths of her falling hair.

"I had to make myself look like a bad thing before she could see me. If I had put on any other shape than a wolf's, she would not have seen me, for that is what is growing to be her own shape inside of her."

They were now climbing the slope of a grassy hill. It was Primrose Hill, in fact, although Diamond had never heard of it. The moment they reached the top, North Wind stood and turned her face toward London. The stars were still shining clear and cold overhead. There was not a cloud to be seen. The air was sharp, but Diamond did not find it cold.

"Now," said the lady, "whatever you do, do not let go of my hand. I might have lost you the last time, only I was not in a hurry then. But now I am in a hurry."

# Chapter Four

# The Little Girl in the Wind

As she stood looking toward London, North Wind was trembling, Diamond saw.

"Are you cold, North Wind?" he asked.

"No, Diamond," she answered, looking down on him with a smile. "I am just getting ready to sweep one of my rooms. Those careless, greedy, untidy children make it into such a mess."

As she spoke he could have told by her voice, if he had not seen with his eyes, that she was growing larger and larger. Her head went up and up toward the stars and as she grew, still trembling through all her body, her hair also grew longer and longer, and lifted itself from her head and went out in black waves. The next moment, however, it fell back around her and she grew smaller again until she was only a tall woman once more. Then she put her hands behind her head and gathered some of her hair and began weaving and knotting it together. When she was done she bent her beautiful face down close to his and spoke.

"Diamond, I am afraid you would not be able to keep hold of me, and I don't want to drop you. So I have been making a place for you in my hair. Come."

Diamond held out his arms like a baby. She took him in her hands, threw him over her shoulder, and said, "Get in, Diamond."

Diamond parted her hair with his hands, crept between, and soon found the little nest she had made for him. It was just like a little pocket, exactly the right size for him. North Wind put her hands to her back, felt all about the nest, and finding it safe, said:

"Are you comfortable, Diamond?"

"Yes, indeed," answered Diamond.

The next moment he was rising in the air. North Wind grew, towering up to the place of the clouds. Her hair went streaming out from her till it spread like a fog over the stars.

Diamond could not help being a little afraid, but he held on tight to the twisted ropes which made his shelter. As soon as he was a little used to it, he peeped through the woven meshes, for he did not dare to look out over the top of the nest. The earth was rushing past like a river below him. Trees and water and grass flew by. A great roar of wild animals rose as they rushed over the zoo, mixed with a chattering of monkeys and a screaming of birds; but it died away in a moment behind them. Now there was nothing but the roofs of houses. Pots fell over and loose pieces flew off the roofs. There was a great roaring, for the wind was dashing against London like the sea. But at North Wind's back Diamond, of course, felt nothing of it all. He was in a perfect calm. He could hear the sound of it, that was all.

By and by he raised himself and looked over the edge of his nest. There were the houses still rushing past. Then he looked up to the sky, but could see no stars. They were hidden by the blinding masses of the lady's hair which swept them. He wondered if she would hear him if he spoke.

"Please, North Wind," he said, "what is that noise?"

From high over his head came the voice of North Wind, answering him gently:

"The noise of my broom. I am the old woman that sweeps the cobwebs from the sky. Only I'm busy with the floor now."

"Why do the houses look as if they were running away?"

"I am sweeping so fast over them."

"I knew London was very big, North Wind. But I didn't know it was as big as this. It seems we will never get away from it."

"We are going round and round, otherwise we would have left it long ago."

"Is this the way you sweep, North Wind?"

"Yes. I go round and round with my great broom."

"Please, would you mind going a little slower, for I want to see the streets."

"You won't see much now."

"Why?"

"Because I have nearly swept all the people home."

"Oh, I forgot," said Diamond, and was quiet after that, for he did not want to be a nuisance.

But she dropped a little toward the roofs of the houses, and Diamond could see down into the streets. There were very few people out.

Suddenly Diamond saw a little girl coming along a street. She was terribly blown about by the wind and was having a difficult time with a broom she was carrying behind her. It seemed as if the wind was angry at her, tearing at her rags.

"Oh, please, North Wind," he cried, "won't you help that little girl?"

"No, Diamond. I mustn't leave my work."

"But why shouldn't you be kind to her?"

"I am kind to her: I am sweeping the bad smells away."

"But you're kinder to me, dear North Wind. Why shouldn't you be as kind to her as you are to me?"

"There are reasons, Diamond. Everybody can't be done to all the same. Everybody is not ready for the same thing."

"But I don't see why you should be kinder to me than her."

"Do you think nothing's to be done but what you can see, Diamond, you silly! Of course you can help her if you like. You've got nothing particular to do at this moment as I do."

"Oh, do let me help her then! But will you be able to wait?"

"No, I can't wait. You must do it yourself. And remember, the wind will get ahold of you too."

"Don't you want me to help her, North Wind?"

"Not without having some idea of what will happen. If you start crying, that won't be of much help to her."

"I want to go," said Diamond. "Only there's just one thing—how am I to get home?"

"If you're worried about that, perhaps you had better stay with me."

"Look!" cried Diamond, who was still watching the little girl. "I'm sure the wind will blow her over. Do let me go."

They had been sweeping more slowly along the line of the street. There was a lull in the roaring.

"Well, though I cannot promise to take you home," said North Wind as she sank nearer and nearer to the tops of the houses, "I can promise you it will be all right in the end. You will get home somehow. Have you made up your mind what to do?"

"Yes—to help the girl," replied Diamond firmly.

The same moment North Wind dropped into the street and stood, only a tall lady now, but with her hair flying up over the housetops. She put her hands to her back, picked Diamond up, and set him down in the street. The same moment he was caught in the fierce blast of the wind and almost blown away. North Wind stepped back a step and at once towered as tall as the houses. Diamond turned to look for the little girl, and when he turned again the lady had vanished, and the wind was roaring along the street as if it had been the bed of an invisible river. The little girl was struggling along, her hair flying too, and behind her she dragged her broom. Her little legs were going as fast as they could to keep from falling.

"Stop! Stop! little girl," shouted Diamond, following her.

"I can't!" wailed the girl. "The wind won't let go of me."

Diamond ran after the girl and in a few moments had caught up with her.

"Where are you going?" he asked.

"Home," she said, gasping for breath.

"Then I will go with you," said Diamond.

They were silent for a while, for the wind blew worse than ever, and they both had to hold on to the lamppost.

"Where do you work?" asked the girl at length; "where is your crossing?"

"I don't sweep," answered Diamond.

"What *do* you do, then?" she asked. "You aren't big enough for most things."

"I don't know what I do," he answered. "Nothing, I suppose. My father's Mr. Coleman's coachman."

"You have a father?" she said, staring at him as if a boy with a father was unusual.

"Yes. Don't you?" returned Diamond.

"No. Nor a mother either. Old Sal's all I've got." And she began to cry.

"I wouldn't go to her if she wasn't good to me," said Diamond.

"But you have to go somewhere."

"Move on," said the voice of a policeman behind them.

"I told you so," said the girl. "You have to go somewhere. They're always after you to move."

"Why are you out so late?" asked Diamond.

"The crossing where I sweep is a long way off at the West End. And now I'm so late getting back old Sal won't open the door."

"You don't mean she won't let you in tonight?"

"It'll be lucky for me if she does."

"We'd better have a try anyhow," said Diamond. "Come along."

As he spoke Diamond thought he caught a glimpse of North Wind turning a corner in front of them. And when they turned the corner too, they found it quiet there, but he saw nothing of the lady.

"Now you lead me," he said, taking her hand, "and I'll take care of you."

The girl withdrew her hand, but only to dry her eyes with her apron. She put it in his again and led him, turning many times, until they stopped at a cellar door in a very dirty street. There she knocked.

"I wouldn't like to live here," said Diamond.

"Oh yes, you would, if you had nowhere else to go to," answered the girl. "I only hope we can get in."

"I don't want to go in," said Diamond.

"Where do you want to go, then?"

"Home to my home."

"Where's that?"

"I don't know exactly."

"Then you're worse off than I am."

"Oh no, for North Wind—" began Diamond, and then stopped.

*"What?"* said the girl, as she held her ear to the door, listening.

But Diamond did not reply. Neither did old Sal.

"I told you so," said the girl. "She is wide awake, listening. But we won't get in."

"What will you do, then?" asked Diamond.

"Move on," she answered.

"Where?"

"Oh, anywhere. I'm used to it."

"Hadn't you better come home with me?"

"That's a good joke, when you don't know where it is. Come on."

"But where?"

"Oh, nowhere in particular. Come on."

Diamond obeyed. The wind had now fallen quite a bit. They wandered on and on, turning in this direction and that, until they got to the end of the houses and were near some fields. By this time they were both very tired. Diamond felt like crying and thought he had been very silly to get down from North Wind's back. He wouldn't have minded if he had been able to do the girl some good, but he thought he had been no use to her. But he was mistaken about that, for she was far happier having Diamond with her than if she had been wandering about alone. She did not seem as tired as he was.

"Let's rest a bit," said Diamond.

"There's something like a railway there," she answered. "Perhaps there's an open arch under it."

They went toward it and found one. But better still there was an empty barrel lying under the arch.

"Here we are!" cried the girl. "A barrel's the jolliest bed of all. We'll have a little nap and then go on."

She crept in and Diamond crept in beside her. They put their arms around each other and when he began to warm up, Diamond's courage began to come back.

"This is nice," he said.

"I can't imagine how a kid like you comes to be out all alone this time of night," said the girl.

She called him a *kid*, but she was really only a month older than he was. But she had to work and that soon makes people older.

"I shouldn't have been out so late if I hadn't got down to help you," said Diamond. "North Wind has probably gone home long ago."

"You said something about the north wind before that I couldn't understand," said the girl. "You must be an idiot."

So now Diamond had to tell her the whole story.

She said she did not believe a word of it. But as she spoke there came a great blast of wind through the arch, which set the barrel rolling. They quickly got out of it and wandered on, sometimes stopping for a rest on a doorstep, but always turning into fields when they had the chance.

At last they found themselves on a rising ground that sloped rather steeply on the other side. Down below, it was bordered by an irregular wall with a few doors in it. The moment they reached the top of the rising ground a gust of wind seized them and blew them downhill as fast as they could run. Diamond could not stop before he went bang against one of the doors in the wall. It burst open and they found themselves looking through the back door of a large garden.

"Ah, ah!" cried Diamond, after staring for a few moments, "I thought so! Here I am in the master's garden. I tell you what, little girl, you just poke a hole in old Sal's wall, and put your mouth to it, and say, 'Please, North Wind, may I go out with you?' and then you'll see what'll happen."

"I daresay I shall. But I'm out in the wind too often already to want more of it."

"I said *with* the North Wind, not *in* it."

"It's all the same."

"It's *not* all the same."

"Yes, it is."

"But I know best."

"And I know better," said the girl. "I'll box your ears if you keep saying that."

Diamond got angry, but he remembered that even if she did box his ears, he mustn't box hers, and all he could do if someone was rude to him was to go away and leave the person. So he went in at the door.

"Goodbye, mister," said the girl. Her calling him *mister* made him forget he was angry.

"I'm sorry I was cross," he said. "Come in and my mother will give you some breakfast."

"No thank you. I must be off to my crossing to sweep. It's morning now."

"I'm very sorry for you," said Diamond.

"Well, it is a life to be tired of—with old Sal, and so many holes in my shoes."

"How can you be so good about it?"

"Oh, it's not so bad. When I think of it I always want to see what's coming next, and so I always wait till next is over. But I suppose there's somebody happy somewhere."

She ran up the hill and disappeared behind it. Then Diamond shut the door as best he could and ran through the kitchen garden to the stable. And how glad he was to get into his own blessed bed again!

# Chapter Five

# The Tulip and the Bumblebee

Diamond said nothing to his mother about his adventure. He half thought that North Wind was a friend of his mother, and that if she did not know all about it, at least she did not mind his going anywhere with the lady of the wind. At the same time he thought it might seem as though he were making up stories if he told everything, especially since he could hardly believe it himself when he thought about it in the middle of the day.

It was some time before he saw the lady of the wind again. Indeed, nothing very unusual happened until the following week. This was what happened then. Diamond the horse needed new shoes, and Diamond's father took him out of the stable, and was just getting on his back to ride him to the blacksmith's when he saw his little boy standing by the pump watching him. Then the coachman took his foot out of the stirrup, let go of the mane and bridle, and lifted up his boy and set him on the horse's back, telling him to sit up straight like a man. He then led away both Diamonds together.

He had not ridden far before Diamond found the courage to

reach forward and take hold of the bridle. And when his father felt the boy pull it toward himself, the coachman looked up and smiled and let go of it, and left Diamond to guide Diamond. And the boy soon found that he could do so perfectly. It was a grand thing to be able to guide a great big animal like that.

The blacksmith lived some distance away, deeper into London. As they crossed the angle of a square, Diamond, who was now quite comfortable on top of Diamond, saw a girl sweeping a crossing for a lady across the street. The lady was his father's employer, Mrs. Coleman, and the little girl was the same one he had walked about with through the night. He drew Diamond's bridle back, slowing down to see whether Mrs. Coleman would give the girl a penny for cleaning off the street for her where she walked. But the lady had just given a penny at the last crossing, so the little girl's hand went back empty to its broom. Diamond had a penny in his pocket, a gift from Mrs. Coleman the day before, and he tumbled off the horse to give it to the girl. She made him a pretty courtsy when he offered the coin, but with a bewildered stare. At first she mused: "Then he *was* on the back of the North Wind after all!" But on looking up at the sound of the horse's feet on the paved crossing, she changed her idea, saying to herself, "North Wind is his father's horse! That is the secret of it!" He smiled at her, and she said, "Thank you, mister. Did they wallop you for being out so late?"

"Oh no," answered Diamond. "They never wallop me."

"Lor!" said the little girl, and was speechless.

In the meantime, Diamond's father had looked behind him and seen the horse's bare back. Then he saw his boy, picked him up again and put him back on.

"Don't get off again, Diamond," he said. "The horse might have stepped on you."

"Yes, Father," he answered.

The summer drew near, warm and splendid. Miss Coleman was in better health and sat in the garden very often. One day she saw Diamond looking through the shrubbery, and called him. He talked to her so plainly that she often sent for him after that, and before long he was allowed to come into the garden whenever he pleased. He never touched any of the flowers or blossoms, for he was not like some boys who cannot enjoy a thing without pulling it to pieces, and so keeping everyone from enjoying it after them.

Even a week is such a long time in a child's life. Diamond had once again begun to feel as if North Wind were only a dream.

One hot evening he had been sitting with the young mistress, as they called her, in the garden. As it grew dusky she began to feel chilled and went in, leaving the boy alone. He sat there gazing at a bed of tulips. Although they had closed for the night, they could not go completely to sleep, for there was a gentle wind that kept waving them about. All at once he saw a great bumblebee fly out from inside one of the flowers.

"There! That is done," said a voice—a gentle, merry, childish voice, but *so* tiny. "I thought he would have to stay inside there all night, poor fellow!"

Diamond could not tell whether the voice was near or far away. It was so small, yet so clear. He had never seen a fairy but he had heard of them, and he began to look around for one. And then he saw the tiniest creature sliding down the stem of the tulip.

"Are you the fairy that takes care of the bees?" he asked, bending down on his knees at the edge of the tulip bed.

"I'm not a fairy," answered the little creature.

"You look very much like one. How am I to know you're not a fairy?"

"In the first place, fairies are much bigger than me."

"Oh," said Diamond thoughtfully. "I thought they were very little."

"But they might be much bigger than I am and still not very big. Why, I could be six times the size I am and not be very huge at all. Besides, a fairy can't grow big and little whenever it wants. Some fairy tales say so, but they don't know better. Come, Diamond! haven't you seen me before?"

As she spoke a breeze of wind bent the tulips almost to the ground and the creature laid her hand on Diamond's shoulder. In a moment he knew it was North Wind.

"I am stupid," he said, "but I never saw you so small before, not even when you were taking care of the primrose."

"Do you have to see me every different size before you know me, Diamond?"

"But how could I think it was you taking care of a big stupid bumblebee?"

"The more stupid he was the more he needed to be taken care of. He was so tired from sucking and trying to open the tulip door. What would the sun have thought when the tulip opened in the morning if instead of seeing the flower's heart, it had found a great big bee lying there?"

"But how do you have time to look after bees?"

"I don't always look after bees. And I don't look after every bee. I had this one to look after, and it was hard work."

"Hard work! Why, you could blow a chimney down—or a boy's cap off," said Diamond.

"Both are easier than to blow a tulip open. That takes such a gentle breath. But I scarcely know the difference between hard and easy. I am always able to do what I have to do. When I see my work, I just go begin it—and then it is done. But I mustn't talk. I have to sink a ship tonight."

"Sink a ship! With people in it?" exclaimed Diamond.

"Yes."

"How dreadful! I wish you wouldn't talk about it."

"It is rather dreadful. But it is my work. I must do it."

"I hope you won't ask me to go with you."

"No, I won't ask you. But you must come anyway."

"But I don't want to. I won't go."

"Won't you?"

And all at once North Wind grew into a tall lady and looked him in the eyes, and Diamond said:

"You may take me. I know you couldn't be cruel."

"No, I could not be cruel even if I wanted to. I can do nothing cruel, although I often do what looks as if it is cruel to those who do not know what I am really doing. They will say I drown people. But the people they say I drown, I only carry away to—to—to—well, to the back of the North Wind—that is what they used to call it long ago, only I never saw the place."

"How can you carry them there if you never saw it?"

"I know the way."

"But how can you never have seen it?"

"Because it is behind me."

"But you can turn around."

"Not far enough to see my own back. No, I always look in front of me. In fact, when I try to see my back I grow quite blind and deaf. So I only pay attention to my work."

"How do you know it is your work?"

"Ah, that I can't tell you exactly. I only know it is. When I do my work I know things are right, and when I don't I feel all wrong. East Wind says—only one does not exactly know how much to believe of what she says, for she can be very naughty sometimes—she says it is all managed by a baby. But whether she is being good or naughty when she says that, I don't know. I just stick to my work. It's all the same to me to let a bee out of a tulip, or to sweep the cobwebs from the sky. Would you like to go with me tonight?"

"I don't want to see a ship sunk."

"But suppose I had to take you?"

"Why then, of course, I would have to go."

"That's a good Diamond.—I think I had better grow a bit first. Only you must go to bed. I can't take you till you're in bed. That's the law about the children. So I had better go and do something else first."

"Very well, North Wind," said Diamond. "What are you going to do first?"

"Jump up on the top of the wall there."

"I can't."

"And I can't help you—you haven't been to bed yet, you see. Now, come out to the road with me, just in front of the coach house, and I will show you."

North Wind grew very small, so small that she could not have blown the dust off a tiny flower. Diamond noted that not even the blades of grass moved as she flitted along by his foot. They left the lawn, went out by the little door in the coach-house gates, and then crossed the road to the low wall that separated it from the river.

"You can get up on this wall, Diamond," said North Wind.

"Yes, but my mother has told me not to."

"Then don't," said North Wind.

"But I can see over it," said Diamond.

"Good. But I can't."

As she said it, North Wind gave a little jump and stood on the top of the wall. She was just about the height a dragonfly would be if it stood on end.

"You little darling!" cried Diamond, seeing what a lovely tiny toy-woman she was.

"Don't be disrespectful, Master Diamond," said North Wind. "If there's one thing that upsets me, it is the way you humans judge things by their size. I am quite as respectable now as I shall be six hours from now when I take a huge ship, twist her around, and push her under. You have no right to address me in such a fashion."

But as she spoke, the tiny face wore the smile of a great, grand woman. "But look there!" she went on. "Do you see a boat with one man in it—a green and white boat?"

"Yes, quite well."

"Can you see the man?"

"He's not a very good rower," said Diamond, "paddling about first with one oar and then the other."

"Now look!" directed North Wind.

And she flashed across the water like a dragonfly. The surface of the water rippled as she passed. The next moment the man in the boat glanced about him and went to work with his oars. The boat went faster over the rippling water. Man and boat and river were awake. Almost the next instant, North Wind perched again on the river wall.

"How did you do that?" asked Diamond.

"I blew in his face," answered North Wind.

"I don't see how that could have done it," said Diamond.

"Therefore you will say you don't believe it could have."

"Oh no, dear North Wind. I know you too well not to believe you."

"Well, I blew in his face and that woke him up."

"What good did that do?"

"Don't you see? Look at him now—how he is pulling the oars. I blew the fog out of his mind."

"How?"

"I cannot tell you that."

"But you did it."

"Yes. I have to do ten thousand things without being able to tell how."

Diamond was staring at the boat, and the next moment North Wind was gone. Away across the river went a long ripple. The man in the boat was putting up a sail. The moon was coming up over the edge of a great cloud. Diamond looked around at it all, then turned back toward the house, put his hands in his pockets, and went in to have his supper. The night was very hot, for the wind had fallen again.

"You don't seem very well tonight, Diamond," his mother commented. "I think you had better go to bed."

"Very well, Mother," he answered.

He stopped for one moment to look out the window. Above the moon the clouds were going different ways and this puzzled him. It looked as if a storm was approaching. He was soon fast asleep.

# CHAPTER SIX

# OUT IN THE STORM

Diamond woke in the middle of the night. All was in darkness. A terrible noise was rumbling overhead, like great drums. The roof of the loft in which he lay had no ceiling. Only the tiles were between him and the sky, and the wind was blowing loud against them. For a while he could not get all the way awake. A peal of thunder burst over his head and he was afraid. He had hardly recovered himself when a great blast of wind tore some tiles off the roof and blew down into his bed. That brought him wide awake and gave him back his courage. The same moment he heard a mighty, yet musical voice calling him.

"Get up, Diamond," it said. "It's all ready. I'm waiting for you." He looked out of the bed and saw a gigantic, powerful, but lovely arm with a hand whose fingers were nonetheless ladylike that they could have strangled a boa constrictor or picked up a tiger. The arm was stretched down through a big hole in the roof. Without a moment's hesitation Diamond reached out his tiny little hand and laid it into the palm of the huge one before him.

The hand felt its way up his arm, grasped it gently and strongly above the elbow, and lifted Diamond from his bed. The moment he was through the hole on the roof, all the winds of heaven seemed to be blowing at him. His hair blew one way, his nightgown another, and he thought his legs were going to blow away from him. Afraid, he held on tightly to the huge hand which held his arm.

"Oh, North Wind!" he cried, but the words vanished from his lips in the noise of the wind, like soap bubbles burst from his little play pipe. And yet North Wind heard his words. When she answered, it seemed to Diamond that she spoke even more tenderly and graciously than before. Perhaps this was because she was so big and because her ears and mouth must seem so dreadfully far away. Her voice was like the bass of a deep organ, without the groan in it; like the most delicate of violin tones, without the wail in it; like the most glorious of trumpet notes, without the defiance in it; like the sound of falling water, without the clatter and clash in it. It was like all of them together, and yet like none of them, for it was even grander. It was more like his mother's voice than anything else.

"Diamond, dear," she said, "be a man. What is fearful to you is not the least fearful to me."

"But it can't hurt you," murmured Diamond, "for you're *it*."

"Then if I'm *it*, and I have you in my arms, how can it hurt you?"

"Oh yes, I see," whispered Diamond. "But it looks so frightening, and the wind pushes me about so hard."

"Yes, it does, my dear. That is what it was sent for."

At the same moment a crash of thunder, which shook Diamond's heart against the sides of his chest, broke from the sky. Diamond had not seen the lightning, for he had been intent on looking for North Wind's face. Every moment the folds of her garment would sweep across his face. But in between, he could just make himself believe that he saw the great woman's eyes looking down at him.

He trembled so at the thunder that North Wind lifted him from the roof high up into the air and held him against her.

"Diamond, dear, this will never do."

"Oh yes, it will," answered Diamond. "I am all right now—quite comfortable. If you will only let me stay here, I shall be all right."

"But you will feel the wind, Diamond."

"I don't mind that, as long as I feel your arms through it," answered Diamond, nestling closer to her.

"Brave boy!" returned North Wind, pressing him closer. "But hadn't you better get into my hair? Then you would not feel the wind. You will here."

"But it is so nice to feel your arms around me. It's a thousand times better to have them, even with the wind, than to have only your hair and the back of your neck and no wind at all."

"But it is surely more comfortable there?"

"Well, perhaps. But I suppose there are better things than being comfortable."

"Yes, indeed there are. Well, I will keep you in front of me. You will feel the wind, but not too much. I shall need only one arm to take care of you. The other will be quite enough to sink the ship."

"Oh, dear North Wind, how can you talk like that?"

"My dear boy, I never just talk. I mean what I say."

"Then you do mean to sink the ship?"

"Yes."

"It's not like you."

"How do you know that?"

"Quite easily. Here you are taking care of a poor little boy like me, using only one arm, and then you talk about sinking a ship with the other. It can't be like you."

"Ah, but which is really *me*? I can't be two me's at once, you know."

"No. Nobody can be two people at once."

"Well, which me is me?"

"I must think about that. There seem to be two."

"But you couldn't know about the thing you didn't know, could you?"

"No."

"Then which me do you know?"

"The kindest, goodest, best me in the world," answered Diamond, clinging to North Wind.

"Why am I good to you?"

"I don't know."

"Have you ever done anything for me?"

"No."

"Then I must be good to you because I choose to be good to you."

"Yes."

"Why should I choose?"

"Because . . . you like to."

"Why would I like to be good to you?"

"I don't know. Unless it's because it's good to be good to me."

"That's just it. I am good to you because I like to be good."

"Then why shouldn't you be good to other people as well as to me?"

"That's just what I am asking you. Why shouldn't I?"

"I don't know. Why shouldn't you?"

"Because I *am* good to other people too."

"But I don't see that you are," said Diamond. "It looks just the opposite."

"Listen to me, Diamond. You know the one *me*, you say, and that is good."

"Yes."

"Do you know the other *me* as well, the one that looks not good?"

"No. I wouldn't like to."

"Well, if you don't know the other me, are you sure of one of them?"

"Yes—the good you."

"And there can't be two me's?"

"No, there can't."

"Then the me you don't know must be the same me as the me you do know."

"Yes . . . I see."

"Then the other me you don't know, the me that looks bad, must not be bad at all but must really be as kind as the me you do know."

"Yes."

"Besides, I tell you that it is so. But I admit it is a little confusing because it doesn't look that way. Do you have any other questions?"

"No, dear North Wind. I am quite satisfied. You may sink as many ships as you like, and I won't say another word. But I don't say I will like to see it, though."

"That's quite another thing," replied North Wind. And as she spoke she gave one jump from the roof of the hayloft and rushed up into the clouds with Diamond on her left arm close to her heart. And as if the clouds knew she had come, they burst into a fresh jubilation of thunderous light.

They were in the midst of the clouds and mists, and it was as if the wind itself had taken shape, and he saw the gray and black wind tossing and raving madly about him. It blinded him by stinging his eyes, and deafened him by bellowing in his ears. And it all quite took his breath away. But he did not mind it. He only gasped at first, then laughed, for the arm of North Wind was about him and he was leaning against her chest. It is quite impossible to describe what he saw. The air and clouds rushed every way at once, wildly twisting and shooting and curling and dodging and clashing madly about. Greater confusion you would see nowhere except in a crowd of frightened people. Diamond saw the threads of the lady's hair streaking in it all. In parts indeed he could not tell what was her hair and what was the black storm clouds. And Diamond felt as if the wind were grabbing his hair, as if he too were part of the storm.

But he was so sheltered in North Wind's arm that he hardly realized how fierce the onslaught really was. For he was carried, nestling in its very core, at the center of it where it all began. It almost seemed to him that they were motionless and that all the confusion was going on around them. Flash after flash of lightning lit up the sky, followed by crash after crash of thunder. But it seemed to Diamond that North Wind and he were motionless, all except for North Wind's swirling hair.

But it was not so. They were sweeping with the speed of the wind itself toward the sea.

Before they reached the sea, Diamond felt North Wind's hair beginning to fall about him.

"Is the storm over, North Wind?" he called out.

"No, Diamond. I am just stopping a moment to set you down. You would not like to see the ship sunk and I am going to find a place for you to wait till I come back for you."

"Oh, thank you," said Diamond. "I shall be sorry to leave you, North Wind, but I would rather not see the ship go down. I'm afraid the poor people will cry and I would hear them."

"There are a good many passengers on board, and to tell you the truth, Diamond, I don't want you to see the ship go down either. I'm afraid it would be a very long time before you would get it out of your little head again."

"But how can you bear it then, North Wind? For I am sure you are kind. I shall never doubt that again."

"I will tell you how I am able to bear it, Diamond. I am always hearing—through every noise, even the noises I make myself—the sound of a far-off song. I do not exactly know where it is, and I don't hear it very loudly, only something like the odor of its music. It comes to me flitting across the ocean outside this air in which I am making such a storm. And the sound of that sweet music is quite enough to make me able to bear the cry from the drowning ship. If you could hear it, it would make you able to bear it too."

"No, it wouldn't," returned Diamond. "For *they* wouldn't hear the far-away song. And even if they did, it would do them no good. You and I are not going to be drowned, and so *we* might be able to enjoy it."

"But you have never heard the song, and you don't know what it is like. Somehow it tells me that all is right, that it is coming to swallow up all the cries. It wouldn't be the song it is if it did not swallow up all their fear and pain too, and set them singing it themselves with the rest. Ever since my hair began to grow out and away, that song has been coming nearer and nearer. Only I must say it was some thousand years before I heard it."

"How can you say it was coming nearer when you did not hear it?" asked doubting little Diamond.

"Since I began to hear it, I know it is growing louder. Therefore, I know it must have been coming nearer and nearer until I was first able to hear it. I am not very old, you know—only a few thousand years—and I was still a baby when I heard the noise first. But I knew it was coming from the voices of people ever so much older and wiser than I was. I can't sing at all, except now and then, and I can never tell what my song is going to be. I only know what it is after I have sung it.—But here is a good place to stop."

"I can't see anything. Your hair is all about me like a darkness and I can't see through it," said Diamond.

"Look, then," said North Wind, and with one sweep of her great white arm, she swept yards of darkness out of the boy's face.

What a blue night it was, lit up with stars. Just opposite Diamond's face the gray towers of a mighty cathedral blotted out the shape of sky and stars.

"What's that?" cried Diamond, for he had never seen a cathedral, as it rose in front of him.

"A very good place for you to wait in," replied North Wind. "But we shall go inside, and you shall decide for yourself."

## Chapter Seven

# The Cathedral

As they swept down out of the sky, North Wind saw an open door in the middle of one of the towers, leading out onto the roof, and through it they flew. Then North Wind set Diamond on his feet, and he found himself at the top of a stone stair which went twisting away down into the darkness inside. There was just barely enough light for Diamond to see that North Wind was standing beside him. He looked up at her face and saw that she was no longer a beautiful giantess, but the tall gracious lady he liked best to see. She took his hand and led him down the spiral stair, through another little door, and out onto a narrow balcony that led all the way around the central part of the church. It was very narrow and there was no railing to keep him from falling into the church, and he held his breath for fear as he looked down.

"What are you trembling for, little Diamond?" asked the lady as she walked gently along.

"I am afraid of falling down there," answered Diamond. "It is so deep and dark."

"Yes, it is," said North Wind. "But you were a hundred times higher a few minutes ago."

"But somebody's arm was about me then," said Diamond.

"It is a pity your sweet little mouth should talk nonsense. Don't you know I have ahold of you?"

"Yes. But I'm walking on my own legs and they might slip. I can't trust myself as well as your arms."

"But I have ahold of you, I tell you, foolish child."

"Yes, but somehow I can't feel comfortable."

"If you were to fall and I should lose my hold on you, I would be down after you in less time than it takes a watch to tick, and catch you long before you had reached the ground."

"I don't like it, though," said Diamond.

*"Oh! oh!"* he screamed the next moment in terror, for North Wind had let go of his hand and had vanished, leaving him standing all alone on the balcony.

She left the words "Come after me" sounding in his ears.

But he dared not move. In a moment more he would, from sheer terror, have fallen into the church. But suddenly there came a gentle breath of cool wind upon his face, and it kept blowing upon him in little puffs, and at every puff Diamond felt courage coming back into his little heart. The cool soft wind kept breathing on him, and the soft wind was so strong in its gentleness that in a minute more Diamond was marching along the narrow ledge as fearless as North Wind herself.

He walked on and on, with the windows all in a row on one side of him and the great empty church on the other, until at last he came to a little open door. There a wider stairway led him down and down and down, till at last all at once he found himself in the arms of North Wind. She held him close and kissed him on the forehead. Diamond nestled up to her and said, "Why did you leave me, dear North Wind?"

"Because I wanted you to walk alone," she answered.

"But it is so much nicer this way," said Diamond.

"But I couldn't hold a coward to my heart. It would make me so cold."

"But I wasn't brave by myself," said Diamond. "It was the wind that blew in my face that made me brave. Wasn't it?"

"Yes, I know that. You had to be taught what courage is. And you couldn't know without feeling it. Therefore, it was given to you. But don't you think that maybe next time you would try to be brave yourself?"

"Yes, I do. But trying is not much."

"Yes, it is—a very great deal, for it is a beginning. And a beginning is the greatest thing of all. To try to be brave *is* to be brave. The coward who tries to be brave is ahead of the man who is brave because he was made that way and never had to try."

"How kind you are, North Wind!"

"I am only just. All kindness is but justice. We owe it."

"I don't quite understand that."

"Never mind. You will someday. There is no hurry about understanding it now."

"Who blew the wind on me that made me brave?"

"I did."

"I didn't see you."

"But you can believe me."

"Yes, of course. But how was it that such a little breath of wind could be so strong?"

"That I don't know."

"But you made it strong."

"No, I only blew it. I knew it would make you strong, just as it did the man in the boat, remember? But how my breath has that power I cannot tell. It was put into it when I was made. That is all I know. But really, I must be going about my work."

"Oh, the poor ship! I wish you would stay here and let the poor ship go."

"I dare not do that. Will you wait here till I come back?"

"Yes. You won't be long?"

"Not longer than I can help. Trust me, you shall get home before morning."

In a moment North Wind was gone, and the next moment Diamond heard a loud moaning about the church. It grew and grew to a great roaring of wind. The storm was up again and he knew that North Wind's hair was flying.

The church was dark. Only a little light came through the windows, which were almost all of stained glass. But Diamond could not see how lovely they were, for there was not enough light to show the colors of them. The church grew very lonely about him, and he began to feel like a deserted child whose mother has forsaken him. But he knew that to be left alone is not always to be forsaken.

He began to feel his way about the place and for a little while went wandering up and down. His little footsteps echoed in the huge house. At length Diamond thought he would like to say something out loud to see if the church would answer him back. But he found he was afraid to speak. Perhaps it was just as well that he did not, for the sound of his own voice echoing in the dark would have made the place feel all the more deserted and empty. But he thought he could sing. He liked to sing and sang at home, making up tunes to all the nursery rhymes he knew. So he began to try *Hey Diddle,* but it wouldn't do. Then he tried *Little Boy Blue,* but it was no better. He tried several others but they all sounded so silly, though he had never thought them silly before. So he remained quiet and listened to the echoes that came out of the dark corners in answer to his footsteps.

At last he gave a great sigh and said, "I'm *so* tired." But he did not hear the gentle echo that answered from far above his head, for at that same moment he stumbled over a step and fell and hurt his arm. He cried a little at first, and then crawled up the steps on his hands and knees. At the top he came to a little bit of carpet, so he lay down on it. And there he lay staring at the darkened window that rose nearly a hundred feet above his head.

It happened to be the eastern window of the church and the moon was just at that moment on the edge of the horizon. In just a few more moments she was peeping over it and began to light up the window which had beautifully colored figures of the Apostles in it. Before long, with the rising of the moon, St. John and St. Paul and the rest of them dawned in the window in their lovely garments. Diamond did not know that the moon was up, and he thought all the light was coming out of the window itself and that the good old men were appearing to help him because he was tired and lonely and had hurt his arm. So he lay and looked at them over his head, wondering when they would come down and what they would do next. They were very dim, for the moonlight was not as strong as the sunlight and he had to look hard to make out their shapes. So his eyes grew tired and then his eyelids grew so heavy that he could not keep them from falling down over his eyes. He kept lifting them up, but every time they felt heavier than the last. In the end it was no use: they were too much for him. In a few moments he gave up trying to keep them up, and the moment he gave it up, he was fast asleep.

That Diamond had fallen asleep is clear from the strange things he now thought were taking place. For he fancied he heard a sound like whispering up in the great window. He tried to open his eyes, but he could not. The whispering went on and grew louder and louder. It was the Apostles talking about him, but he could not open his eyes.

"How did he come to be lying there, St. Peter?" said one.

"I think I saw him a while ago up in the gallery, under the Nicodemus window. Perhaps he fell down. What do you think, St. Matthew?"

"I don't think he could have crawled here after falling from such a height. He must have been killed."

"What are we to do with him? We can't leave him lying there. And we could not make him comfortable up here in the window. It's rather crowded already. What do you say, St. Thomas?"

"Let's go down and look at him."

Then came a rustling and a chinking for some time, and then there was silence, and Diamond felt that all the Apostles were standing around him and looking down on him. But still he could not open his eyes.

"What's the matter with him, St. Luke?" asked one.

"There's nothing the matter with him," answered St. Luke, who must have joined the company of the Apostles from the next window. "He's in a sound sleep."

"I have it!" cried another. "This is one of North Wind's tricks. She has dropped him at our door like an orphan baby. I don't understand that woman's conduct, I must say. As if we didn't have enough to do without having to take care of other people's children! That's not what our forefathers built cathedrals for."

Now Diamond could not stand to hear such things against North Wind. She would never play a trick on anybody. She was far too busy with her own work for that. He struggled hard to open his eyes, but without success.

"She should consider that a church is not a place for pranks, not to mention that *we* live in it," said another.

"It certainly is disrespectful of her. But she is always disrespectful. What right does she have to bang at our windows as she has been doing this whole night? I bet there is broken glass somewhere. I know my blue robe is in a dreadful mess with the rain first and then the dust. It will cost me shillings to clean it."

Then Diamond knew they could not be Apostles talking like this. They could only be sextons and gardeners and such who got up at night and put on robes and called each other grand names. And he was so angry at their daring to say those things about North Wind that he jumped up.

"North Wind knows best!" he cried. "She has a good right to blow the cobwebs from your windows, for she was sent to do it. She sweeps them away from grander places, I can tell you, for I've been with her while she does."

This was what he started to say, but as he spoke his eyes opened wide. For there were no Apostles or churchmen there at all—not even a stained-glass window, but only a dark pile of hay all about him, and in the little panes in the roof of his loft was the glimmering blue light of the morning. Old Diamond was coming awake down below in the stable. In another moment he was on his feet and shaking himself so much that young Diamond's bed trembled under him.

"I wish I could shake myself like that," said Diamond. "But then I can wash myself and he can't. What a picture it would be to see old Diamond trying to wash himself with his hoofs!"

He got up and dressed himself. Then he went out into the garden. There must have been a tremendous wind during the night, for the great elm tree had crashed to the ground. Diamond almost cried to see the wilderness of green leaves, which used to be tossing about in the breeze so far up in the blue air, now lying so near the ground without any hope of ever getting up into the air again.

*I wonder how old the tree is,* thought Diamond. "It must take a long time to get so near the sky as that poor tree was."

"Yes, indeed," said a voice beside him, for Diamond had spoken the last words aloud.

Diamond jumped, and looking around saw a minister, a brother of Mrs. Coleman, who happened to be visiting her. He was a great scholar and liked to get up early.

"Who are you, my man?" he added.

"Little Diamond," answered the boy.

"Oh. I have heard of you. Why are you up so early?"

"Because the pretend Apostles talked such nonsense they waked me up."

"You must have been dreaming, my little man," said the minister. "Dear, dear!" he went on, looking at the tree, "there has been terrible work here. This is the north wind's doing. What a pity! I wish we lived at the back of it."

"Where is that, sir?" asked Diamond.

"Away in the north, beyond the mountains," answered the minister, smiling.

"I never heard of the place," returned Diamond.

"I suppose not," said the minister. "But if this tree had been there now, it would not have been blown down, for there is no wind there."

The minister looked very kindly at Diamond as he turned away toward the house. And Diamond thought to himself, *I will ask North Wind next time I see her to take me to that country. I think she did speak about it once before.*

# Chapter Eight

# How Diamond Got to the Back of the North Wind

When Diamond went in for breakfast, he found his father and mother already seated at the table. They were both busy with their bread and butter, and Diamond sat down in his usual place. His mother looked up at him, watched him a moment, and then spoke.

"I don't think the boy is looking well, Husband."

"Don't you? I don't know. I think he looks well enough. How do you feel, Diamond, my boy?"

"Quite well, thank you, Father. Except I've got a little headache."

"There, I told you," said his father and mother both at once.

"The child's very poorly," said his mother.

"The child's quite well," added his father.

Then they both laughed.

"I've got a letter from my sister at Sandwich," said his mother, "and she wants the boy to go down to see her."

"And that is why you want to think he isn't looking well."

"He's looking better now. I suppose he could go."

"Well, I don't care, if you can find the money," said his father.

"I'll manage that," his mother responded. And so it was agreed that Diamond should go to Sandwich to visit his aunt.

I will not describe the preparations Diamond made. Nor will I describe the journey. When he arrived he was met at the train station by his aunt, a cheerful middle-aged woman. She took him into the sleepy old town while Diamond stared about with his beautiful big eyes at the quaint old streets and shops and houses.

Diamond soon made great friends with an old woman who ran a toy shop, for his mother had given him a few cents for pocket money before he left. He had gone into her shop to spend it, and she had got talking to him. She looked very funny because she didn't have any teeth, but Diamond liked her and went to her shop often, although he had nothing to spend there after his few cents were gone.

One afternoon he had been wandering rather wearily about the streets for some time. It was a hot day and he was tired. As he passed the toy shop he stepped inside.

"Please may I sit down for a minute on this box?" he asked, thinking the old woman was somewhere in the shop. But he got no answer, and sat down anyway. Around him were a great many toys of all prices. All at once he heard a gentle whirring somewhere among them. He looked behind him and there were the sails of a windmill going round and round. At first he thought it must be one of those toys which are wound up and go by some kind of mechanism inside. But no, it was a plain penny toy, with the windmill at the end of a whistle, and when the whistle blows the windmill goes. But the strange thing was that there was no one at the whistle end blowing to make it go, and yet the sails were turning round and round.

"What can it mean?" mused Diamond aloud.

"It means me," said the tiniest voice he had ever heard.

"Who are you?" asked Diamond.

"Well, really," said the voice. "I am beginning to be surprised at you. I wonder how long it will take before you know me. You are just like a baby who doesn't know its mother because she has on a new hat."

"Not quite so bad as that, dear North Wind," said Diamond, "for I didn't see you at all; and indeed I don't see you yet, although I recognize your voice. Can't you grow a little, please?"

"Not a hairsbreadth," said the voice, and it was the smallest voice that ever spoke. "What are you doing here?"

"I came to visit my aunt. But, North Wind, why didn't you come back for me in the church that night?"

"I did. I carried you safely back home. All the time you were dreaming about the glass Apostles, you were lying in my arms."

"I'm so glad," said Diamond. "I thought that must be it, only I wanted to hear you tell me. Did you sink the ship, then?"

"Yes."

"And drown everybody?"

"Not quite. One boat got away with six or seven men in it."

"How could the boat swim when the ship couldn't?"

"Of course I had some trouble with it. I had to improvise a bit, and manage the waves a little to keep the lifeboat afloat. When men are thoroughly waked up, I sometimes have a good deal of trouble with them. They're apt to get stupid and tumble over one another's heads. However, the boat got to a desert island before noon the next day."

"And what good will come of that?"

"I don't know. I obeyed orders. Goodbye."

"Oh, North Wind, *do* stay!" cried Diamond, dismayed as he saw the windmill getting slower and slower.

"What is it, my dear child?" asked North Wind, and the windmill began to turn again so swiftly that Diamond could hardly see it.

"I want you to take me to the country at the back of the north wind."

"That's not so easy," said North Wind, and was silent for so long that Diamond thought she had gone. But after he had given up on her, the voice began again.

"I almost wish the old Greek writers had never said anything about it. Much *they* knew! Then that minister would not have set you wanting to go. But we shall see. Now you must go home, my dear, for you don't seem very well. I'll see what can be done for you. Don't wait for me. I've got to break a few of old Goody's toys. She's thinking too much of her new stock. Two or three will do. There! go now."

Diamond rose without a word, left the shop, and went home.

It soon appeared that his mother had been right about him, for that same afternoon his head began to ache very badly and he had to go to bed.

He awoke in the middle of the night. The window of his room had blown open and the curtains around his little bed were swinging about in the wind.

*If that should be North Wind now!* thought Diamond.

But the next moment he heard someone closing the window, and his aunt came to his bedside. She put her hand on his face and said, "How's your head, dear?"

"Better, Auntie, I think."

"Would you like something to drink?"

"Oh yes, I would, please."

So his aunt gave him some lemonade and Diamond felt very much refreshed. He laid his head down again to go back to sleep. But he came awake again as another burst of wind blew the window open a second time. The same moment he found himself in a cloud of North Wind's hair, with her beautiful face bending over him.

"Quick, Diamond!" she said. "I have found a chance!"

"But I'm not well," said Diamond.

"I know that, but you will be better when you have had a little fresh air. And you shall have plenty of that."

"You want me to go, then?"

"Yes, I do. It won't hurt you."

"Very well," replied Diamond. He got out of his bed and jumped into North Wind's arms.

"We must hurry before your aunt comes," she said as she glided out of the window and left it swinging.

The moment Diamond felt her arms fold around him he began to feel better. It was a moonless night and very dark, with glimpses of stars through the clouds. Looking down Diamond saw the white glimmer of waves breaking on the seashore far below him.

"You see, Diamond," said North Wind, "it is very difficult for me to get you to the back of the north wind, for that country lies in the very north itself, and of course I can't blow northward."

"Why not?" asked Diamond.

"You little silly," said North Wind. "Don't you see that if I were to blow northward, I would be South Wind. The north wind always comes *from* the north."

"But how can you ever get home, then?"

"You are quite right—that is my home, though I never get farther than the outer door. I sit on the doorstep and hear the voices inside. I am nobody there, Diamond."

"I'm very sorry."

"Why?"

"That you should be nobody."

"Oh, I don't mind it. Dear little man! You will be very glad someday to be nobody yourself. But you can't understand that now, and you had better not try, for if you do you'll probably make yourself miserable about it."

"Then I won't," said Diamond.

"That's a good boy. It will all come in good time."

"But you haven't told me how you get to the doorstep."

"It's easy enough for me. I have only to consent to be nobody, and there I am. I draw into myself and there I am on the doorstep. But you can see that to drag you along, as heavy as you are, would take centuries, and I couldn't give that much time to it."

"I'm sorry I'm so heavy for you. I would be lighter if I could, but I don't know how."

"You silly darling. Why, I could toss you a hundred miles if I liked. It is only when I am going home that I find you heavy."

"Then are you going home with me?"

"Of course. That is why I came to fetch you."

"But all this time you must be going southward."

"Yes, I am."

"Then how can you take me northward?"

"A very sensible question. I will show you. But I must get rid of a few of these clouds—they come up so fast! There, now it's clear below. What do you see now?"

"I think I see a little boat way down there."

"A little boat indeed! She's a huge yacht, and the captain is a friend of mine. He is a man of good sense and can sail his ship well. I've helped him many times when he didn't even realize it. I've heard him grumbling at me when I was doing the very best for him I could. Why, I've carried him eighty miles a day, many times, due north."

"He must have had to zigzag to do that," said Diamond, who had been watching the ships and had seen that they went other ways than the direction the wind was blowing by going back and forth against it, and by turning their sails.

"Of course he must. But don't you see I was doing all I could. I couldn't be South Wind. And besides, it gave him part of the responsibility himself. Remember, Diamond, it's not good to do everything for those you love and not give them a share in the doing. If I had been South Wind, the captain would only have smoked his pipe all day, and made himself stupid."

"But how could he be a man of sense if he grumbled at you when you were doing your best for him?"

"You must make allowances for people," said North Wind, "or you will never do justice to anybody.—But you do understand, don't you, that a captain may sail north—"

"In spite of a north wind—yes," answered Diamond.

"Not *in spite of,* my dear," said North Wind. "But with the north wind's help. For suppose the north wind wasn't blowing at all? Where would he be then?"

"Then the south wind would carry him."

"So you think that when the north wind stops, the south wind blows. Nonsense. If I didn't blow, the captain couldn't sail his eighty miles a day. No doubt South Wind would carry him faster, if she was blowing straight behind him. But if she was not blowing and if I stopped, there would be a dead calm. So he does not sail north in spite of me; he sails north with my help. Do you see that, Diamond?"

"Yes I do, North Wind. I am stupid, but I don't want to be."

"Good boy! I am going to blow you north in that little boat, one of the finest that ever sailed the sea. Here we are, right over it. I will be blowing against you, you will be sailing against me, and everything will be fine. The captain won't go as fast as he would like, but he will get on, and so shall we. I'm going to put you on board. Do you see in front of the tiller—that thing the man is working, now to one side, now to the other—a round thing like the top of a drum?"

"Yes," said Diamond.

"Below that is where they keep their spare sails. I am going to blow that cover off and right at that moment drop you onto the deck. You must jump into that place. Don't be afraid. It is not deep and you will fall on sailcloth. You will find it nice and warm and dry—but dark. And you will know I am near you by every roll and turn of the ship. Curl yourself up and go to sleep. The ship will be my cradle and you will be my baby."

"Thank you, dear North Wind. I am not a bit afraid," said Diamond.

In a moment they were down to the ship's level, and North Wind sent the hatch rattling and then off. The next moment Diamond found himself in the dark, for he had tumbled through the hole as North Wind had told him, and the cover was immediately replaced over his head. He went rolling about, for the wind began to blow very hard. He heard the call of the captain and the loud trampling of the men over his head as they hauled at the main sail. Diamond felt about until he found what seemed the most comfortable place, and there he snuggled down.

A great many hours went by, and still Diamond lay there. He never felt tired or impatient, for a strange pleasure filled his heart. All the sounds blended together—the straining of the rope masts, the splashing and thudding of the waves against the ship's sides, the roaring of the wind, and the shouts of the men. It was all part of the grand music his North Wind was making about him to keep him from getting tired as they sped on toward the country at the back of her doorstep.

How long this lasted Diamond had no idea. He seemed to fall asleep sometimes, although even through the sleep he could still hear the sounds going on. At length the weather seemed to get worse. The confusion and trampling of feet grew more frequent over his head and the banging and thumping of the waves and the roaring of the wind seemed to be fighting angrily against the ship. All at once a terrible uproar arose. The hatch was blown off, a cold fierce wind swept in where he lay, and a long arm came in which laid hold of him and lifted him out. Almost the next instant he saw the ship far below him. A short distance to the south lay a much larger vessel and toward it North Wind was carrying Diamond. It was a German ship, on its way to the North Pole.

"That ship down there will give us a lift now," said North Wind. "And after that I must do the best I can."

She managed to hide him among the flags of the big ship, which were all snugly stowed away, and on and on they sped toward the north. Finally one night she whispered in his ear, "Come on deck, Diamond."

He got up at once. Everything looked very strange. Here and there on all sides were huge masses of floating ice, looking like cathedrals and castles and crags, while beyond them was a blue sea.

Some of the icebergs were drifting northward. One was passing very near the ship. North Wind seized Diamond and with a single jump landed on one of them. The same instant a wind began to blow from the south. North Wind hurried Diamond down the north side of the iceberg, stepping by its sharp jags, for this berg had never gotten far enough south to be melted and smoothed by the summer sun. She brought him to a cave near the water. She entered it, let go of Diamond's hand, and sat down on a ledge of ice as if weary.

Diamond sat himself on the other side. The cave was a deep, dazzling blue inside, a deeper, lovelier blue than the deepest blue of the sky. But when he looked across to North Wind he was frightened. Her face was worn and white.

"What is the matter with you, dear North Wind?" he asked.

"Nothing much. I feel very faint. But you mustn't mind me, for I can bear it quite well. South Wind always blows me faint. If it were not for the cool of the thick ice between me and her, I should faint altogether. Indeed, as it is, I fear I am about to vanish."

Diamond stared at her in terror, for he saw that her form and face were slowly growing transparent, as if she were dissolving, not in water, but in light. He could see the opposite sides of the cave right through her. Before long all he could see was her pale face with two great clear eyes in it.

"Does it hurt you?" asked Diamond.

"It is very uncomfortable," she answered. "But I don't mind it, for I will be all right before long. I thought I would be able to go with you all the way, but I cannot. Don't be frightened, though. Just go on straight and you will get there all right. You will find me on the doorstep."

As she spoke her face too faded away, only Diamond thought he could still barely see her eyes shining through the blue. When he went closer, however, he found that what he thought were her eyes were only two hollows in the ice. North Wind was gone, and Diamond would have cried if he had not trusted her so much. So he sat still in the blue air of the cave, listening to the ripple of the water all about the iceberg. A light south wind was blowing, the current was moving north, and he went quite fast.

After a little while Diamond went out and sat on the edge of his floating island and looked down into the ocean beneath him. As the time passed he felt as if he were in a dream. When he got tired of the green water, he went back into the blue cave; and when he got tired of the blue cave, he went back out and gazed all about him on the sea sparkling in the sun. Mostly he gazed northward to see if any land was appearing. All this time he never felt hungry. Every now and then he broke off little bits of the berg and sucked them, and he thought they tasted very nice.

At length, one time he came out of his cave and far off on the horizon he saw a shining peak that rose high into the sky. The closer they got to it the higher the peak rose and Diamond began to see other peaks rising about it. He thought this must be the place he was going to. And he was right. At last he saw the line of the coast, and the iceberg floated right into a little bay. All around were huge mountains with snow on their tops. Diamond stepped on shore, and without looking behind him, he began to follow a natural path which wound toward the top of the mountain.

The air was very cold, and seemed somehow dead, for there was not the slightest breath of wind. Finally he reached a high plateau, with mountains shooting up on all sides. In the center of the ridge in front of him there was a gap like the opening of a valley. As he walked toward it he saw the form of a woman seated against the ice in front of the valley, leaning forward with her hands in her lap, and her hair hanging down to the ground.

"It is North Wind on her doorstep," said Diamond joyfully, and hurried on. He soon came to the place, and there she sat, like a huge Egyptian statue, motionless, with drooping arms and head. Diamond grew frightened because she did not move or speak. He was sure it was North Wind, but he thought she must be dead. Her face was white as the snow, her eyes were blue as the air in the ice cave, and her hair hung down straight, like icicles.

He stood in front of her and gazed fearfully into her face for a few moments. Finally with a trembling voice he said, "North Wind."

"Yes, child," said the form, without lifting its head.

"Are you sick, dear North Wind?"

"No. I am waiting."

"For what?"

"Till I'm wanted."

"Don't you care for me anymore?" said Diamond, almost crying.

"Of course I do. But I can't show it. All my love is down at the bottom of my heart. But I feel it bubbling there."

"What do you want me to do next, dear North Wind?" asked Diamond.

"What do you want to do yourself?"

"I want to go to the country at your back."

"Then you must go through me."

"I don't know what you mean."

"I mean just what I say. You must walk on as if I were an open door, and go right through me."

"But that will hurt you."

"No it won't. But it will hurt you."

"I don't mind that, if you tell me to do it."

"Do it," said North Wind.

Diamond walked toward her. When he reached her knees, he put out his hand to touch her, but nothing was there except an intense cold. He walked on. Then all became very white around him and the cold stung him like fire. He walked on. The whiteness thickened all about him and finally he lost all sense of direction. He felt as if he were fainting, swallowed up in whiteness. It was when he reached North Wind's heart that he fainted and fell. But as he fell, he rolled over the doorway behind her.

And that was how Diamond got to the back of the north wind.

## Chapter Nine

# At the Back of the North Wind

Now I have come to the most difficult part of the story. It is very difficult to describe the country at the back of the north wind. And when Diamond came back, he had forgotten a great deal, and what he did remember was very hard to tell. Things there are so different from things here. For one thing, the people there do not speak the same language. Indeed, Diamond insisted that they do not speak at all.

Everyone who has been there describes the country differently. One man reported that he had to enter that country through a fire hotter than boiling glass instead of through ice, as had been the case with Diamond. A peasant girl, on the other hand, fell fast asleep in a wood and woke in that same country. The man who had gotten to the back of the north wind through fire said that everything smelled sweet, and that a gentle, even-tempered wind always breathed in his face. He also described a little river with the purest water in the world. To him it always seemed like the month of May in that country, everything green and fresh, and all the people free and just and healthy.

A shepherd told the story of the peasant girl's travels to the back of the north wind, writing it in a poem, part of which went like this:

> She spoke of the lovely forms she had seen,
> And a land where sin had never been;
> A land of love and a land of light,
> Without sun, or moon, or even night;
> Where the river flowed a living stream,
> And the light a pure and cloudless beam:
> The land of vision it would seem,
> And still an everlasting dream.

As for Diamond himself, when he woke up, North Wind herself was nowhere to be seen. Neither was there any snow or ice within sight. Even the sun had vanished, but there was still plenty of light. Where the light came from he never found out. Sometimes he thought it came out of the flowers, which were very bright. He said the river—for everyone agrees that there is a river there—flowed in a channel of grass instead of over rocks, pure meadow grass which was not too long. Diamond insisted that it sang as it went, singing tunes right into people's heads. After this Diamond was often heard singing, and when he was asked what he was singing, he would answer, "One of the tunes the river at the back of the north wind sang."

He could not say he was completely happy there, for he did not have his father or his mother with him. But he felt so still and quiet and patient and contented that it was even better than mere happiness. Nothing went wrong at the back of the north wind. Neither was everything completely right either, he thought. Only everything was going to be right someday.

When he was asked whether he saw anybody he knew there, he answered, "Only a little girl belonging to the gardener, who thought he had lost her, but was quite mistaken, for there she was safe enough. She was to come back someday, as I came back, if they would only wait patiently."

"Did you talk to her, Diamond?"

"No. Nobody talks there. They only look at each other and understand everything."

"Is it cold there?"

"No."

"Is it hot?"

"No."

"What is it, then?"

"You never think about such things there."

"What a strange place it must be!"

"It's a very good place."

"Do you want to go back again?"

"No. I don't think I have left it. I feel it here, somewhere."

"Did the people there look pleased?"

"Yes—quite pleased, only a little sad."

"Then they didn't look glad."

"They looked as if they were waiting to become gladder someday."

This was how Diamond used to answer questions about that country. And now I will take up the story again, and tell you how he got back to this country.

## Chapter Ten

# How Diamond Got Home Again

When someone at the back of the north wind wanted to know how things were going with anyone he loved, he had to go to a certain tree, climb up it, and sit down in the branches. In a few minutes, if he kept very still, he would see something of what was going on with the people he loved.

One day when Diamond was sitting in this tree, he began to want very much to get home again, for he saw his mother crying. But how was he to get started? He had not seen North Wind, ever since he came. The moment he had gotten to her back, she was completely gone from his sight. He had never seen her back. She might still be sitting on her doorstep looking southward, and waiting, white and thin and blue-eyed, until she was wanted. Or maybe she was a mighty wind again, flying far away with great power. But he could not go home without her, and therefore he must find her.

In his anxiety about his mother, Diamond climbed the tree every day to sit in its branches. One day he was looking southward. Far away he saw a blue shining sea, dotted with gleaming and sparkling specks of white. *Those must be the icebergs!* Nearer by he saw a great range of snow-capped mountains, and down below him the lovely meadow grass of the country, with the stream flowing and flowing through it, away toward the sea. Now he could see that the country was surrounded by a ridge of ice, and in the distance he thought he could just make out the vapory form of North Wind, seated just as he had left her, on the other side. Quickly he descended the tree and found that the whole country had shrunk and now lay like a map at his feet. With a single stride he had crossed the river, with another he had reached the ridge of ice, and with a third he stepped over the ice peaks and sank wearily down at North Wind's knees. For there she sat on her doorstep. The peaks of the great mountains of ice were as high as ever once again behind her, and the country at her back had disappeared from Diamond's view.

North Wind was as still as Diamond had left her. Her pale face was white as the snow and her motionless eyes were as blue as the caverns in the ice. But the instant Diamond touched her, her face began to change as if she were waking from a sleep. Light began to glimmer from the blue of her eyes. In another moment she laid her hand on Diamond's head and began to touch his hair. Diamond took hold of her hand and laid his face to it.

"How very alive you are, child!" she murmured. "Come nearer."

He clambered up beside her and laid himself on her. She gave a great sigh, slowly lifted her arms, and slowly folded them around him until she held him close. In another moment she roused herself and came quite awake. The cold of her chest, which had gone straight to Diamond's bones, vanished.

"Have you been sitting here ever since I went through you, dear North Wind?" asked Diamond, stroking her hand.

"Yes," she answered, looking at him with her old kindness.

"Aren't you very tired?"

"No. I've often had to sit longer. Do you know how long you have been away?"

"Oh, years and years!" answered Diamond.

"You have just been seven days," returned North Wind.

"I thought it had been a hundred years!" exclaimed Diamond.

"I daresay," replied North Wind. "You've been away from here seven days. But how long you may have been in there is quite another thing. Behind my back and in front of my face the time may be quite different. They don't go by the same rules at all."

"I'm glad," said Diamond after a while.

"Why?" asked North Wind.

"Because I've been there such a long time, and yet it won't seem so long to my mother. Why, she won't even be expecting me home from Sandwich yet!"

"No. But we mustn't talk any longer. I've got my orders now, and we must be off in a few minutes."

The next moment Diamond found himself sitting alone on the rock. North Wind had vanished. A creature like a little bumblebee flew past his face, but there were no insects in this icy region. It passed him again and again, flying in circles around him. Finally he realized it must be North Wind herself. But she was no longer vapory and thin. She was solid, but very tiny. In another moment she perched on his shoulder.

"Come along, Diamond," she said in his ear in the smallest and highest of voices. "It is time we were setting out for Sandwich."

"Won't you take me in your arms and carry me?" he said.

"Ah, you ungrateful boy," returned North Wind. "Yes, I will carry you, but you will have to walk a bit first."

She jumped from his shoulder, but when Diamond looked for her on the ground, he could see nothing but a little spider with long legs that made its way over the ice toward the south. It ran very fast indeed for a spider, but Diamond ran ahead of it, then stopped to wait for it. By the time it had caught up with him, it had grown a good deal bigger. The spider kept growing bigger and bigger and going faster and faster, till all at once Diamond discovered that it was not a spider, but a weasel. And away went the weasel, and away went Diamond after it. He had to run as fast as he could to keep up with it. Then the weasel grew and grew and grew, till all at once Diamond saw that the weasel was not a weasel, but a cat. And away went the cat, and Diamond after it. And when he had run half a mile, he found the cat waiting for him, sitting up washing her face. Away went the cat again, and Diamond after it. But the next time he caught up to the cat, the cat was not a cat, but a leopard. And the leopard grew into a jaguar, all covered with spots. And the jaguar grew into a great tiger. Yet Diamond was not afraid of any of them, for he had been at North Wind's back, and he could never be afraid of her again whatever she did or whatever she grew into. And the tiger flew over the snow in a straight line for the south, growing smaller and smaller to Diamond's eyes till it was only a black speck in all the whiteness. Then it disappeared altogether. By this time Diamond was very tired and thought he would rather not run any farther. He slowed to a walk and said aloud to himself:

"I know North Wind will come back, for I can't go much farther without her."

"You dear boy! It was only in fun. Here I am!" said North Wind's voice behind him.

Diamond turned and saw her as he liked best to see her, standing beside him, a tall lady.

"Where's the tiger?" he asked. "But, of course," he added, "you were the tiger. I forgot. I saw it so far ahead of me, and then here you were behind me. It's odd, you know."

"It must look very odd to you, Diamond. But it is no more odd to me than to break an old pine tree in two."

"Well, that's odd enough," returned Diamond.

"So it is. I forgot. Well, none of these things are odder to me than it is for you to eat bread and butter."

"I would like a slice of bread and butter. It's been so long since I had anything to eat."

"Come then," said North Wind, stooping and holding out her arms. "You shall have some bread and butter very soon. I am glad to hear you want some."

Diamond held up his arms to meet hers and was soon safe against her bosom. North Wind jumped into the air. Her robes began to rise and flow and spread out, and with a roar her hair streamed out behind her, the waves rose at their feet, and Diamond and North Wind went flying swiftly southward.

As they flew, they went so fast that the sea slid away under them till all the colors of blue and gray and green mixed together. The stars blurred together overhead and Diamond went fast asleep in North Wind's arms. When he woke, a face was bending over him, but it was not North Wind's. It was his mother's. He put out his arms to her, and she clasped him to herself and burst out crying. Diamond kissed her again and again to make her stop. Perhaps kissing is the best thing for crying, but it will not always stop it.

"What is the matter, Mother?" he said.

"Oh, Diamond, my darling! you have been so sick!" she sobbed.

"No, Mother dear. I've only been at the back of the north wind," returned Diamond.

"I thought you were dead," said his mother.

Just at that moment the doctor came in.

"Oh good!" said the doctor with gentle cheerfulness. "I see we're better today."

Then he drew the mother aside and told her not to talk to Diamond or to pay much attention to what he might say, for he must be kept as quiet as possible. And indeed Diamond did not feel much like talking, for he felt very strange and weak, which was little wonder since all the time he had been away he had only sucked a few lumps of ice, and there could not be much nourishment in them.

Now while he lay there getting strong again with chicken broth and other nice things, I will tell you what had been taking place at his home.

You may remember that Miss Coleman was in a poor state of health. There were three reasons for this. In the first place, her lungs were not strong. In the second place, there was a man who had not behaved very kindly to her. In the third place, she didn't have very much to do. Of course the first of these things she could not help. And the second she couldn't quite help. And if she had tried to find something worth doing, these first two causes wouldn't have made her sick all by themselves. I admit it is not always easy to find something to do that is worth doing, but she might have found something if she had tried. Her fault lay in that she had not tried. So she just went day after day with nothing to do, and all three things together made her sick. Her father and mother were somewhat to blame, for they had never set her going in the direction of doing anything worthwhile. But no one had told them they ought to set her going in that direction. So as none of them would find it out by themselves, North Wind had to teach them.

That night when North Wind left Diamond in the cathedral, she had been very busy helping the Colemans. Miss Coleman's maid had accidentally left a part of her mistress's window open, and the girl's health was considerably worse the next morning. And the ship which North Wind had sunk that night belonged to Mr. Coleman. It was a very heavy loss for him because things had not been going well in his business for some time and he had been getting poorer and poorer. It is a hard thing for a rich man to become poor. But it is not nearly so bad a thing to become poor as it is to become dishonest. Actually, a man may be worth a great deal more when he is poor than when he was rich. But dishonesty is a terrible thing whether a man is poor or rich. And since Mr. Coleman had been growing dishonest, North Wind had to look after him and try to make an honest man out of him. So she sank the ship, which was his last investment, and he was what he and his wife and the world called ruined financially.

And this was not all. For Miss Coleman's lover was a passenger on board the ship. And when the news came that the ship had sunk and that everyone on board had drowned, she was all the more grief-stricken, and that made her sickness worse yet.

Of course the trouble did not end with Mr. Coleman and his family. Nobody suffers completely alone. When a man brings money troubles on himself by trying to get rich too quickly, then most of the people around him must suffer in the same way with him. Therefore the fall of Mr. Coleman also crushed the little family that lived over his coach house and stable. Before Diamond was well enough to be taken home, there was no home for him to go to. The people whom Mr. Coleman owed money to had sold the house, the carriage, the horses, the furniture, and everything. He and his wife and daughter and Mrs. Crump had gone to live in a small house where he could walk to his place of business in the city, hoping yet to retrieve his fortunes. Let us hope he lived long enough to recover his honesty once again too.

Of course, Diamond's father did not have anything to do for a while, but it was not so hard for him to have nothing to do as it was for Miss Coleman. He wrote to his wife in Sandwich that it would be better if she could stay with her sister till he found another place for them. Diamond's aunt was quite willing to keep them as long as she could. And indeed Diamond was not yet well enough to be moved with safety.

When he had recovered enough to be able to go outside, one day his mother got her sister's husband, who had a pony cart, to carry them down to the seashore for a little while. He had some business to do and would pick them up a few hours later when he was ready to return. The sea air would do them both good, she said, and besides, she thought it would be easier for her to tell Diamond about what had happened if she was alone with him.

CHAPTER ELEVEN

# THE SEASIDE

Diamond and his mother sat down on the edge of the grass that bordered the sand. The sun was just far enough past its highest not to shine in their eyes when they looked eastward. A sweet little wind blew on their left side and comforted the mother without letting her know what it was that comforted her. Away in front of them stretched the sparkling waters of the ocean. In both directions from where they sat, the shore rounded outward, forming a little bay. There were no white cliffs here, as farther north and south. It was all flat and not a house or another person was within sight. Dry sand was about their feet, and growing out from it was thin, wiry grass.

"Oh dear!" said Diamond's mother with a deep sigh, "it's a sad world."

"Is it?" said Diamond. "I didn't know."

"How would you know, child? You've been too well taken care of, I trust."

"Oh yes, I have," returned Diamond. "I'm sorry. I thought you were taken care of too. I thought Father took care of you. I will ask him about it. I think he must have forgotten."

"Dear boy!" said his mother. "Your father's the best man in the world."

"I thought so," returned Diamond. "I was sure of it!—Well, doesn't he take very good care of you?"

"Yes, yes, he does," answered his mother, bursting into tears. "But who's to take care of him? And how's he to take care of us if he's got nothing to eat himself!"

"Oh dear!" said Diamond, "hasn't he got anything to eat?"

"No, no, child. It isn't that bad yet. But what's to become of us I don't know."

"I don't understand you at all, Mother," said Diamond. "What's the matter?"

"There are people in the world who have nothing to eat, Diamond."

"Do they—they—what you call—die—then?"

"Yes, they do. How would you like that?"

"I don't know. I never tried."

"Poor boy! How little you know about things! Mr. Coleman has lost all his money and your father has no job now, and we shall all have nothing to eat by and by."

"Are you sure, Mother?"

"No, thank Heaven! I'm not sure of it."

"There's a piece of gingerbread in the basket, Mother."

"Oh you little bird! You have no more sense than a sparrow that picks what it wants and never thinks of the winter and the frost and the snow."

"But the birds get through the winter, don't they?"

"Some of them fall dead on the ground."

"They must die sometime. They wouldn't want to be birds forever. Would you, Mother?"

*What a child he is!* thought his mother, but she said nothing.

"Father told me one day that the rose bushes, and the may bushes, and the holly bushes were the birds' barns, and they stored up food for them for the winter."

"Yes, that's all very true. But there are no such barns for you and me, Diamond."

"Aren't there?"

"No, we've got to work for our bread."

"Then let's go to work," said Diamond, getting up.

"It's no use. We have nothing to do."

"Then let's wait."

"Then we shall starve."

"No we won't. There's the basket there with our lunch in it. I've always had plenty to eat. I've heard you say I had too much sometimes."

"But that's because there's a cupboard I've kept with food in it for you."

"And when yours was empty, Auntie opened hers."

"But that can't go on."

"How do you know? I think there must be a big cupboard somewhere out of which all the little cupboards are filled, you know, Mother."

"Well, I wish I could find the door of that cupboard," said his mother. Then she stopped and was silent for a long time. She had heard something at church the day before about only eating for today and not for tomorrow. So instead of saying anything more, she opened the basket and she and Diamond had their lunch.

Diamond did enjoy it. The drive and the fresh air had made him quite hungry. But he didn't like his mother worrying about what they would eat. He had lived so long without any food at all at the back of the north wind that he knew quite well that food was not essential to existence.

His mother did not speak much as they ate. Afterward she helped him to walk about a little, though he was not able to do much and soon got tired. But he was glad to have the sun and the wind about him again. He lay down in the dry sand, and his mother covered him up with her shawl. She then sat by his side and took a bit of work from her pocket. But Diamond felt rather sleepy, and turned over on his side and gazed sleepily over the sand. A few yards off he saw something fluttering.

"What is that, Mother?" he asked.

"Only a bit of paper," she answered.

"It flutters more than a bit of paper would, I think," said Diamond.

"I'll go and see if you like," said his mother.

She rose and went and found that it was a little book, partly buried in the sand. But several of the pages were out of the sand

and the wind was blowing them about. She picked it up and brought it to Diamond.

"What is it, Mother?" he asked.

"Some nursery rhymes, I think," she answered.

"Would you read some of them to me?"

"Yes," she said, and began one. —"But this is such nonsense!" she said again. "I will try to find a better one."

She turned the pages, searching, but three times, with sudden puffs, the wind blew the pages back to the same verses.

"Do read that one," said Diamond, who seemed to be thinking just the same as the wind was. "I'm sure it is a good one."

So his mother began, though she couldn't find any sense in it. And I do not know exactly what the mother read, but this is what Diamond thought afterward that he had heard. He was, however, very sleepy. And when he thought he understood the verses, he may only have been dreaming better ones. This is something like how they went, although it was much longer than this:

I know a river
whose waters run asleep
run ever
singing in the shallows
quiet in the hollows
sleeping so deep
and all the swallows
that dip their feathers
in the hollows
or in the shallows
are the merriest swallows of all
and the buttercups are growing
beside the flowing
of the singing river
always and ever
growing and blowing
and the sheep beside them
are the quietest sheep
awake or asleep

with the merriest bleat
and the little lambs
are the merriest lambs
with the whitest wool
and the longest tails
and they shine like snow
in the grasses that grow
by the singing river
that sings for ever
and the sheep and the lambs
are merry for ever
because the river
sings and they drink it
and the sweetest wind
blows by the river
flowing for ever
but you never can find
from whence comes the wind
that blows on the hollows
and over the shallows
where dip the swallows
alive it blows
the life as it goes
awake or asleep
into the river
that sings as it flows
and the life it blows
is the life of the river
flowing for ever
that washes the grasses
still as it passes
and feeds the daisies
the little white praises
and buttercups bonny
so golden and sunny
with butter and honey
that whiten the sheep
awake or asleep

it's all in the wind
that blows from behind
and all in the river
that flows for ever.

Here Diamond became aware that his mother had stopped reading.

"Why don't you go on, Mother dear?" he asked.

"It's such nonsense!" said his mother. "I believe it would go on forever."

"That's just what it did," said Diamond.

"What did?" she asked.

"Why, the river. That's almost the very tune it used to sing."

His mother thought his fever was coming on again, so she said nothing.

"Who wrote that poem?" asked Diamond.

"I don't know," she answered. "Some silly woman for her children, I suppose."

"She must have been at the back of the north wind some time or another," said Diamond. "She couldn't have done it anywhere else. That's exactly how it went."

And he began to chant bits of it here and there. But his mother said nothing for fear of making his fever worse. And she was very glad indeed when she saw her brother-in-law jogging up in his little horse-drawn wagon. They lifted Diamond in and got up themselves, and away they went, "home again, home again," as Diamond sang.

But he soon grew quiet, and before they reached Sandwich he was sound asleep and dreaming of the country at the back of the north wind.

CHAPTER
TWELVE

# A NEW HOME AND AN OLD FRIEND

After this Diamond began to recover very fast, and in a few days he was quite able to go home. Back in London his father had come across a new plan to provide for his family. He had a friend in the Bloomsbury region who rented out cabs and horses to the cabmen who then took people about London to earn their living. He happened to meet this man one day as he was returning from an unsuccessful application for a job, and he said to Diamond's father:

"Why don't you go into business for yourself—as a cab driver, I mean?"

"I've saved up a little money," answered Diamond's father. "But I haven't enough for that."

"Well, come home with me and look at a horse I can let you have cheap. I bought him a few weeks ago thinking he'd be a good horse for a Hansom, but I was wrong. He ain't fast enough for that, for he ain't as young as he once was. But for a slow four-wheeled wagon to take families and their luggage about, he's the perfect horse. He's a strong one, just slow. I bought him cheap, and I'll sell him cheap."

"But there's the cab too," said Diamond's father. "It would take a good deal of money to get set up in the business for myself."

"I could fit you with a cab too, I daresay," said his friend. "But come and look at the animal, anyhow."

"Since I lost my old pair, that were Mr. Coleman's," said Diamond's father, going with him, "I don't have the heart to look another horse in the face. No one should part a man and his horse."

But imagine his delight when he went into the stable with his friend and found that the horse that was for sale was none other than his own old Diamond, who had grown very thin and bony.

"*He* ain't a Hansom horse," said Diamond's father indignantly.

"Well, you're right there. He ain't handsome, but he's a good one," said his owner.

"Who says he ain't handsome? He's one of the handsomest horses a gentleman's coachman ever drove," said Diamond's father.

"Well," said his friend, "all I can say is that here's just the animal for you, as strong as a church."

But Diamond's father could say nothing, for he had a lump in his throat and tears in his eyes. On hearing his voice, the horse had turned his long neck around, and when his old friend went up to him, old Diamond whinnied for joy. That settled the matter. The coachman's arms were round the horse's neck in a moment and he almost broke down and cried. And his friend must have been a good-hearted fellow, for instead of adding something to the price he had wanted to get for old Diamond because he was now pretty sure of selling him, he actually took a pound off what he had meant to ask, saying to himself it was a shame to part old friends. So the end of it was that Diamond's father bought old Diamond again, along with a four-wheeled cab. And as there were some rooms for rent above the stable, he took them, wrote to his wife to come home, and was soon set up in business for himself as a cabman.

I have been so full of Diamond that I forgot to tell you that a new baby had arrived in the meantime. It was late in the afternoon when Diamond and his mother and the baby reached London. His father was waiting for them with his own cab, and especially after seeing who the horse was, Diamond was beaming with pride to ride home in his father's own carriage. But when they got to the mews, which is what the stables were called, he could not help being a little dismayed at first, and if he had not been to the back of the north wind I am afraid he would have cried a little. For to have to change houses was bad enough, but it was a rather dreary place and the weather was depressing, for a thick, dull, persistent rain was falling by the time they reached home. But happily the weather is changeable, and besides, the room was warm and cheery from a good fire, which their neighbor had built for them. And with a good fire, and tea and bread and butter, things cannot be too miserable.

It was indeed a change to them all. Instead of the great river which they had been able to see from the Colemans', their windows now looked out upon a dirty paved yard. And there was no garden now for Diamond to run into when he pleased, with gay flowers about his feet and sun-filled trees over his head. Neither was there a wooden wall at the back of his bed with a hole in it for North Wind to come in at when she liked. Indeed, there was such a high wall about the stables, and there were so many houses about the mews that North Wind seldom got into the place at all. And the partition at the head of Diamond's new bed only divided it from the room occupied by a cabman who drank too much beer and came home to quarrel with his wife and pinch his children. It was dreadful to Diamond to hear the scolding and the crying. But it could not make him miserable, because he had been at the back of the north wind. And whenever Diamond began to feel a kind of darkness or depression spreading over him, he said to himself, "This will never do. I can't give in to this. I've been to the back of the north wind. Things go right there, so I must try to get things to go right here. I've got to fight the miserable things.

They won't make me miserable if I can help it."

If you find it hard to believe that Diamond should be so good, you must remember that he had been to the back of the north wind.

# Chapter Thirteen

# Diamond's First Day at the Mews

The first night at Diamond's new home the wind blew loud, but Diamond slept deep and never heard it. There were many such times when he slept well and remembered no dreams or anything else when he woke in the morning. I think that on those nights Diamond went to the back of the north wind. I am almost sure that was how he woke so refreshed and felt so quiet and hopeful all the day. Indeed, when he woke from such a sleep there was a something in his mind, he could not tell what—something like the last far-off sounds of the river dying away in the distance, or some of the words of the endless song his mother had read to him on the seashore. Sometimes he thought it must have been the twittering of the swallows—over the shallows, you know; but it *may* have been the chirping of the dingy sparrows picking up their breakfast in the yard outside his room—I don't know. When Diamond knew he was coming awake, he would sometimes try hard to keep hold of the words of the song, but always as he came *awaker*—as he would say—one line faded away, and another, and then another, till at last there was nothing left but some lovely picture of water or grass or daisies. And then the next day he would sing the oddest, loveliest little songs to the baby—of his own making, his mother said; but Diamond said he did not make them. They were made somewhere inside him, and he knew nothing about them till they were coming out.

When he woke that first morning he got up at once and went into his mother's room. He found her lighting the fire, and his father just getting out of bed. They had only one room besides the tiny one in which Diamond slept. He decided he had been sick long enough and set about to be more help. His mother was looking gloomy and his father was silent, and if Diamond had not done all he could possibly do to keep out the misery that was trying to get in at the doors and windows of their cheerless new home, he too would have grown miserable. But to try to make others comfortable is the only way to be comfortable ourselves, and that comes of not being able to think so much about ourselves when we are helping other people. For our Selves will always do pretty well if we don't pay them too much attention.

"Why, Diamond, child!" said his mother, "you're so good to me—taking care of the baby while I get breakfast ready, and sweeping up the hearth! I declare one would think you had been among the fairies."

Diamond merely smiled sweetly to her and sat down again and took the baby on his lap and began poking his face into its little body, laughing and singing so that before long the baby was laughing too. And what he sang was something like this—such nonsense to those who couldn't understand it, but not to the baby, who got all the good in the world out of it:

Baby's a-sleeping
wake up, baby,
for all the swallows
are the merriest fellows
and have the yellowest children
who would go sleeping and snoring
disturbing his mother
and father and brother
and all a-boring
their ears with his snoring

wake up, baby,
hark to the gushing
hark to the rushing
where the sheep are the woolliest
and their tails the whitest
and baby's the bonniest
and baby's the funniest
and baby's the tiniest
and baby's the merriest
of all the lambs
whose mothers are the whitest
that feed the lambs
and father's the best
of all the swallows
that build their nest
out of the shining shallows
and he has the merriest children
that's baby and Diamond
and Diamond and baby
and baby and Diamond
and Diamond and baby.

Then Diamond's knees went off in a wild dance, which tossed the baby about and shook the laughter out of him. His mother had been listening to the last few lines of his song, and came in with tears in her eyes. She took the baby from him, gave him a kiss, and told him to run to the table.

When his father had finished his breakfast, which he did rather in a hurry, he got up and went down into the yard to get out his horse and put him to the cab.

"Won't you come and see the cab, Diamond?" he said.

"Oh yes, Father, I almost forgot," said Diamond. "And old Diamond too?"

"Yes, of course."

When Diamond got down into the yard he noticed how thin old Diamond looked, with his bones pushing through his skin. But when he came round in front of him, the old horse began sniffing at him and rubbing his horsey upper lip and nose on him; and then Diamond did just as his father had done—he put his arms round old Diamond's neck and cried.

"Was there ever anybody so lucky as me, Father?" he said. "Dear old Diamond!" He hugged the horse again, and kissed both his big hairy cheeks. In the meantime his father fastened Diamond's harness to the cab, then mounted the coach box.

"Oh, Father, do let me drive a bit," said Diamond, jumping up on the box beside him.

His father changed places with him at once, putting the reins into his hands. Diamond gathered them up eagerly.

"Don't pull at his mouth," said his father. "Just feel at it gently to let him know you're there and attending to him. That's what I call talking to him through the reins."

"Yes, Father, I understand," replied Diamond. Then to the horse he said, "Come on, Diamond." And old Diamond's ponderous bulk began at once to move to the voice of the little boy.

But before they had reached the entrance of the mews, another voice called after them.

"Husband," said Diamond's mother, coming up behind them, "you're not going to trust *him* with the reins so soon?"

"He must learn someday," replied Diamond's father, "and he can't begin too soon. Anyone can see he's a born coachman," he added proudly, "just like my father and my grandfather before him. Besides, old Diamond's as proud of him as we are ourselves, just waiting to hear his words and obey them."

"Well, I can't do without him today. There's so much to be done. It's my first day here, and the baby!"

"Bless you, Wife! I never meant to take him away—only to the end of Endell Street. He can walk back."

"No thank you, Father. Not today," said Diamond. "Mother needs me. Perhaps she'll let me go another day."

"Very well, my man," replied his father, and took the reins which Diamond was holding out to him.

Diamond got down, a little disappointed of course, and went in with his mother who was too pleased to speak. She took his hand and held it tight, glad that he did not want to leave her.

Now, although they did not know it, the owner of the stables, the same man who had sold the horse to Mr. Coleman, had been standing just inside one of the stable doors and had heard and seen this whole incident. And from that day on John Stonecrop took a great liking to the little boy.

That very evening, just as Diamond was feeling tired from the day's work and wishing his father would come home, Mr. Stonecrop knocked at the door. Diamond's mother went and opened it.

"Good evening, ma'am," he said. "Is the little master in?"

"Yes, to be sure—at your service, Mr. Stonecrop."

"No, ma'am, it's I who am at his service. I'm just going out with my own cab, and if he wants to come with me, he can drive my old horse."

"It's getting rather late for him," said his mother thoughtfully. "You see, he's been an invalid."

Diamond wondered how he could have been an invalid when he did not even know what the word meant. But of course his mother must be right.

"Well," said Mr. Stonecrop, "I could just let him drive to Bloomsbury Square and then he could run home from there."

"Very good, sir," said his mother. And dancing with delight, Diamond got his cap, put his hand in Mr. Stonecrop's, and went with him to the yard where the cab was waiting. He did not think the horse looked nearly so nice as Diamond, nor Mr. Stonecrop nearly so grand as his father. But he was nonetheless pleased. He got up on the box, and his new friend got up beside him.

"Careful of the gate," said Mr. Stonecrop as he handed Diamond a whip and they set off. Diamond did mind the gate and guided the horse through it in safety, pulling him this way and that according to what was necessary. Diamond learned to drive all the sooner that he was in the habit of doing just as he was told and could obey the smallest hint in a moment. Some people don't know how to do what they are told. Because they are not used to it, they neither understand quickly nor are able to turn what they do understand into action quickly. But with an obedient mind one learns the rights of things fast enough, for it is the law of the universe, and to obey is to understand.

"Look out!" cried Mr Stonecrop as they were turning the corner into Bloomsbury Square.

It was getting dusky and a cab was approaching rather rapidly from the opposite direction. Pulling aside, and the other driver stopping, they only just escaped a collision. Then they each saw the other.

"Why, Diamond, it's a bad beginning to run into your own father!" cried the driver.

"But, Father, wouldn't it have been a bad ending to run into your own son?" said Diamond in return, and the two men laughed heartily.

"It's very kind of you, Mr. Stonecrop, to take him out with you," said Diamond's father.

"He's a brave fellow, and will be fit to drive on his own in a week or two. But I think you'd better let him drive you home now, for his mother didn't want him to have too much of the night air and I promised not to take him farther than the square."

"Come along then, Diamond," said his father as he brought his cab alongside the other, and moved to make room for Diamond to jump across to his own box. "Good night, Mr. Stonecrop." As they drove away, Diamond felt more like a man than he had ever yet had a chance of feeling in all his life.

# Chapter Fourteen

# The Young Cabbie

Diamond soon became a great favorite with all the men about the mews. Some may think it was not the best place for him to be brought up in, but it must have been, for there he was. At first he heard a good many rough and bad words, but he did not like them and so they did not stick to him and get inside him. Thus they did him no harm. He never took any notice of them, and his face shone pure and good in the middle of it all, like a primrose in a hailstorm. At first, because his face was so quiet and sweet and always with a smile on it, they said he wasn't all there, meaning that he was half an idiot. But actually he was a great deal more there than they had the sense to see. And before long the bad words found themselves ashamed to come out of the men's mouths when Diamond was near. When they talked to him nicely he always had a good answer ready, sometimes a smart one, and that helped to make them change their minds about him.

One day one of the stable hands named Jack gave him a currycomb and a brush to try on old Diamond's coat. He used them so well and so gently, yet so thoroughly, as far up the horse's sides as he could reach, that the man could not help admiring him.

"You must grow taller," he said. "It won't do to have a horse's belly clean and his back dirty, you know."

"Help me up," said Diamond, and in a moment he was on the old horse's back with the comb and brush. He sat there and curried and brushed as the horse ate his hay, first moving the comb and brush along one side of his neck, and then on the other. When that was done he asked for a dressing comb and combed old Diamond's mane thoroughly. Then he did the horse's shoulders and back and sides. Finally he turned round and tried to comb Diamond's tail. But this was not so easy, for he had to lift it up, and every now and then old Diamond would whisk it out of the boy's hands, and once he sent the comb flying out of the stable door, to the great amusement of the men. But Jack fetched it for Diamond again, and he began once more and did not stop till he had done the whole business fairly well. All the time the old horse went on eating his hay, and, except for an occasional whisk of his tail, seemed to take no notice of all that was going on. But he was just pretending not to notice, for of course he knew very well who it was that was perched on his back and rubbing away at him with the comb and brush. So he was quite pleased and proud, and perhaps thought to himself something like this: *I'm a stupid old horse, who can't brush his own coat. But there's my young godson on my back, cleaning me like an angel.*

I won't vouch for what the old horse was thinking, for it is very difficult to find out what any old horse is thinking.

"Oh dear," said Diamond when he was through, "I'm tired." He laid himself down at full length on old Diamond's back.

By this time all the men in the stable were gathered about the two Diamonds, and all much amused. One of them lifted the boy down, and from that time on he was a greater favorite with them than before. Before long they even came to argue among themselves about who should have Diamond with them, and, though he went mostly with his father, and though his mother did not always like the idea of his going out with the other men, he did learn to drive all sorts of horses through the most crowded streets of London. He never got frightened and never let himself get in too great a hurry. Yet when the moment came for doing something quickly, he was always ready for it. I must once again remind you that he had been to the back of the north wind and that is how he was able to learn to do things so skillfully.

One day his father took him on his own cab. After a stray job or two they drew up in the row for cab horses on Cockspur Street. They waited a long time but nobody seemed to want to be carried anywhere. But after a while there would be ladies going home from the Academy exhibition, and then there would be the chance of a job.

"Though, to be sure," said Diamond's father, "some ladies is very hard, and keeps you to the bare sixpence a mile, when everyone knows that ain't enough to keep a family on."

Since it was very hot, Diamond's father got down to get something to drink. He left Diamond up on the box. Suddenly there was a noise in the street and Diamond looked around to see what was the matter.

There was a crossing near the cab stand where a girl was sweeping. Some rough young imps had picked a fight with her and were now trying to get her broom away from her.

Diamond jumped down and ran to help the girl. He got hold of the broom and pulled with her. But this just made the boys get all the rougher, and one of them hit Diamond on the nose and made it bleed. But since he could not let go of the broom to take care of his nose, he was soon a mess. Presently his father came back, and, seeing Diamond in the middle of the tumult, rushed in and sent the boys flying in all directions. The girl thanked Diamond and began sweeping again as if nothing had happened, while his father led him away. With the help of the old waterman, the boy was soon washed up and looking decent again. His father set him up on the coach again, perfectly satisfied with the account he gave of himself.

A moment later, up came the girl, running with her broom over her shoulder and calling, "Cab, there! Cab!"

Diamond's father turned instantly, for his cab was first in line, and followed the girl. When they reached the curbstone, who should be waiting for them but Mrs. and Miss Coleman! They did not look up at the cabman, however. The girl opened the door for them; they gave her the address, and a penny. She told the cabman, and away they drove.

When they reached the house, Diamond's father got down and rang the bell. As he opened the door of the cab, he touched his hat. The ladies both stared for a moment, and then exclaimed together, "Why, Joseph! Can it be you?"

"Yes, ma'am; yes, miss," he answered, again touching his hat, with all the respect he could possibly put into the action. "It's a lucky day for me to see you again."

"Who would have thought it?" said Mrs. Coleman. "Times have changed for us both, Joseph, and it's not very often we can even afford to have a cab now. But you see my daughter is still very poorly. Indeed, we meant to walk a bit first before we took a cab, but just at the corner a cold wind came down the street, and I saw that she shouldn't be out in it. But to think we should have met you, of all the cabmen in London! I didn't know you had a cab of your own."

"Well, you see, ma'am, I had a chance of buying the old horse, and I couldn't resist *him*. There he is, looking at you, ma'am. Nobody can tell the sense in that head of his."

The two ladies went near to pat the horse, and then they noticed Diamond up on the box.

"Why, you've got both Diamonds with you," said Miss Coleman. "How are you, Diamond?"

Diamond lifted his cap and answered politely.

"What's your fare, Joseph?" asked Mrs. Coleman, taking out her purse.

"No thank you, ma'am," said Joseph. "It was your own old horse that brought you home. And me you paid long ago."

He jumped up onto the box of the coach before she could say another word, and with a parting salute drove off, leaving them on the sidewalk.

It had been quite a while now since Diamond had seen North Wind, or even thought much about her. And as his father drove along, Diamond was not thinking about her so much as he was the crossing sweeper, and was wondering what made him feel as if he knew her quite well. Then a picture rose in his mind of a little girl running before the wind and dragging her broom after her, and by degrees he recalled the whole adventure of the night when he got down from North Wind's back in a London street. But he could not quite satisfy himself whether the whole thing had not been a dream which he had dreamed when he was a very little boy. Only he had been to the back of the north wind since then—there could be no doubt of that, for when he woke every morning, he always knew that he had been there again.

And as he thought and thought, he recalled another thing that had happened that very morning, which, although it seemed to be merely an accident, might have something to do with what had happened since. His father had intended to go to the stand at King's Cross that morning, and had turned into Gray's Inn Lane to drive there. But they found the way blocked and were told that a stack of chimneys had been blown down in the night and had fallen across the road. They were just clearing the rubbish away. Diamond's father had turned, made for Charing Cross, and that is how they happened to see the little girl and the Colemans.

That night the father and mother had a great deal to talk about.

"Poor things!" said the mother. "It's worse for them than it is for us. They've been used to such grand things, and for them to have to move to a tiny little house like that must be sad."

"Is it a disgrace to be poor?" asked Diamond, who had been listening and did not understand the tone in which his mother had spoken.

But his mother, whether conscience-stricken I do not know, instead of answering him, hurried him away to bed, where he lay trying to understand until he was at last conquered by invading sleep.

## Chapter Fifteen

# Diamond's Friends

One day when old Diamond was standing with his nose in his feed bag between Pall Mall and Cockspur Street, and his master was reading the newspaper on the box of his cab, little Diamond got down to stretch, for his legs were getting tired of sitting. He walked up to the crossing where the girl and her broom were to be found in all kinds of weather. Just as he was going to speak to her, a tall gentleman stepped onto the street. He was pleased to find it so clean, for the streets were muddy and he had nice boots on. So he put his hand in his pocket and gave the girl a penny for keeping the crossing so nice. She gave him a sweet smile in return, and made him a pretty curtsey, and he looked at her again, and said:

"Where do you live, my child?"

"In Paradise Row," she answered.

"Whom do you live with?"

"My wicked old grannie," she replied.

"You shouldn't call your grannie wicked," reproved the gentleman.

"But she is," said the girl, looking up confidently in his face. "If you don't believe me, you can come and take a look at her."

The words sounded rude, but the girl's face looked so simple that the gentleman saw she did not mean to be rude, and he became even more interested in her.

"Still, you shouldn't say so," he insisted.

"Shouldn't I? Everybody calls her a wicked old grannie. You should hear her swear."

The gentleman looked very grave, for he was sorry that such a nice little girl should be in such bad keeping. But he did not know what to say next and stood for a moment with his eyes looking down at the ground. When he lifted them, he saw the face of Diamond looking up in his.

"Please, sir," said Diamond, "her grannie's very cruel to her sometimes and shuts her out in the streets at night if she happens to be late."

"Is this your brother?" asked the gentleman of the girl.

"No, sir."

"How does he know your grandmother then? He does not look like one of her sort."

"Oh no, sir. He 's a good boy—quite a good one, if you know what I mean."

Here she tapped her forehead with her finger in a significant manner.

"What do you mean by that?" asked the gentleman, while Diamond was looking on.

"The cabbies call him God's baby," she whispered. "He's not right in the head, you know. He's not quite all there. A tile loose."

Still Diamond kept smiling, though he understood every word. What could it matter what people called him so long as he did nothing he shouldn't? And besides, to be called "God's baby" was surely the best of names!

"Well, my little man, and what can you do?" asked the gentleman, turning toward him.

"Drive a cab," said Diamond.

"Good. And what else?" he continued, for, believing what the girl had said, he took the still sweetness of Diamond's face as a sign that he wasn't quite normal and wanted to be kind to the poor child.

"Take care of a baby," said Diamond.

"Well—what else?"

"Clean my father's boots and make a bit of toast for his tea."

"You're a useful little man," said the gentleman. "What else can you do?"

"Not much that I know of," said Diamond. "I can't curry a horse unless somebody puts me on his back. So I don't count that."

"Can you read?"

"No, but Mother and Father can, and they're going to teach me."

"Well, here's a penny for you."

"Thank you, sir."

"And when you have learned to read, come to me, and I'll give you a sixpence and a book with nice pictures in it."

"Please, sir, where am I to come?" asked Diamond, who was too much a man of the world not to know that he must have the gentleman's address before he could go to see him.

*You're no such silly after all!* thought the gentleman as he put his hand in his pocket and brought out a card. "There," he said, "your father will be able to read that and tell you where to go."

"Yes, sir. Thank you, sir," said Diamond, putting the card into his pocket.

The gentleman walked away, but turning around for one last look, he saw Diamond give his penny to the girl.

"Is she as cruel as ever?" Diamond asked her when the man was gone.

"Much the same. But I gets more coppers now than I used to and can get something to eat, and still take enough home besides to keep her from grumbling. It's a good thing she's so blind, though."

"Why?" asked diamond

"'Cause if she was as sharp in the eyes as she used to be, she would find out I never eats her food, and then she'd know I get something somewheres and would know I don't give her all the money."

"Doesn't she watch you?"

"'Course she do. But I just pretend and then drop it into my lap and then scoop it into my pocket."

"What would she do if she found you out?"

"She'd never give me no more."

"But you don't want it."

"Yes, I do want it."

"Why?"

"To take to Cripple Jim."

"Who's Cripple Jim?"

"A poor boy in the Row. He's not much, but he's a good boy and I love him dearly. I always keeps a penny for Jim—leastways as often as I can. But, look out, I must sweep again, for them buses makes no end o' dirt."

"Diamond! Diamond!" cried his father, who was afraid he might get no good talking to the girl. Diamond obeyed and went to him and climbed back up on the box. He told his father about the gentleman and what he had promised him if he would learn to read, and showed him the gentleman's card.

"Why, it's not far from the mews!" said his father, giving him back the card. "Take care of it, my boy, for it may lead to something. God knows, in these hard times a man needs as many friends as he's likely to get."

"Haven't you got enough friends, Father?" asked Diamond.

"Well, I have no right to complain. But the more the better, you know."

"Just let me count," said Diamond.

He took his hands from his pockets, spread out the fingers of his left hand, and began to count, beginning at the thumb.

"There's Mother first, and then baby, and then me. Next there's old Diamond and the cab—no, I won't count the cab, for it never looks at you, and when Diamond's not hooked to its shafts, then it's nobody at all. Then there's the man that drinks next door, and his wife, and his baby."

"They're no friends of mine," said his father.

"Well, they're friends of mine," said Diamond.

His father laughed. "Well, go on," he said.

"Then there's Jack and Mr. Stonecrop, and not to mention Mr. Coleman and Mrs. Coleman and Miss Coleman, and Mrs. Crump. And then there's the clergyman that spoke to me in the garden a long time ago that day the tree was blown down."

"What's his name?"

"I don't know his name."

"Where does he live?"

"I don't know."

"How can you count him, then?"

"He did talk to me, and very kindly too."

His father laughed again.

"Why, child, you're just counting everybody you know. That doesn't make them friends."

"Doesn't it? I thought it did. Well, they shall be my friends. I shall make them my friends."

"How can you do that?"

"Well, if I choose to be their friend, they can't prevent me. Like that girl at the crossing."

"A fine set of friends you'll have, Diamond."

"Surely *she's* a friend, Father. If it hadn't been for her, you wouldn't have got to take Mrs. Coleman and Miss Coleman home."

His father was silent, for he saw that Diamond was right and was ashamed to find himself more ungrateful than he had thought.

"Then there's the new gentleman," Diamond went on.

"If he does as he says," interposed his father.

"And why shouldn't he? But I don't quite understand, Father; is nobody your friend but the one who does something for you?"

The father's heart was fairly touched now. He made no answer and Diamond ended by saying:

"And there's the best of mine yet to come—and that's you, Daddy, except it be Mother, you know. You're my friend, Daddy, aren't you? And I'm your friend, aren't I?"

"And God for us all," said his father, and then they were both silent, for that was very solemn.

# Chapter Sixteen

# Sal's Nanny

The question of the tall gentleman as to whether Diamond could read or not set his father thinking it was high time the boy could. And as soon as old Diamond was fed, the father began the task that very night. But it was not much of a task to Diamond, for his father took for the lesson book that same book of rhymes his mother had picked up at the seashore. And since Diamond had not begun too soon, he learned very fast indeed. Within a month he was able to sound out most of the verses for himself.

But he had never come upon the poem he thought he had heard his mother read from the book that day. He had looked through it several times after he knew the letters and a few words, thinking he could tell the look of it. But he had not found it.

For three days Diamond did not see the girl at her crossing, and he became quite anxious about her, fearing she must be ill. On the fourth day, still not seeing her, he said to his father, who had just at that moment shut the door of his cab on a fare:

"Father, I want to go and see about the girl. She can't be well."

"All right," said his father. "Only take care of yourself, Diamond."

So saying, he climbed up on the cab and drove off, while Diamond walked down the street. He had great confidence in his boy, and would trust him anywhere. But if he had known the kind of place in which the girl lived, he would perhaps have thought twice before he allowed him to go alone. From talking to the girl Diamond had a good idea where it was, and he remembered the address well enough. So by asking his way some twenty times, mostly of policemen, he finally got near the place. The last policeman he questioned looked down upon him from his height of six feet, two inches, and replied with another question, but kindly:

"Why do you want to go there? It's not where you was bred, I'd say."

"No, sir," answered Diamond. "I live in Bloomsbury."

"That's a long way off," said the policeman.

"Yes, it's a good distance," answered Diamond. "But I can find my way pretty well, and policemen are always kind to me."

"But what on earth do you want here?"

Diamond told him plainly what he was doing, and of course the man believed him, for no one ever disbelieved Diamond.

"It's an ugly place," said the policeman.

"Is it far off?" asked Diamond

"No, it's close by. But it's not safe."

"Nobody hurts me," said Diamond.

"I must go with you."

"Oh, please don't," said Diamond. "They might think I was bringing you around to do them some harm."

"Well, as you please," said the man, and gave him the directions he needed. Diamond set off, never suspecting that the policeman—who was a kindhearted man with children of his own—was following him and watching him close around every corner. As Diamond went, all at once he thought he remembered the place, and whether he did or was only following the policeman's instructions, he went straight for the door of old Sal.

"He's a sharp little kid anyhow, for as simple as he looks, he didn't take a single wrong turn," said the man to himself. "But old Sal's a rum 'un for such a child to pay a morning visit to. She's worse when she's sober than when she's half drunk. I've seen her when she'd have torn him in pieces."

Happily for Diamond, old Sal had gone out to get more to drink. When he came to her door, in a cellar at the bottom of a stair, he knocked but received no answer. He put his ear to the door and thought he heard a moaning inside. He tried the door, found it was not locked, and went inside. It was a dreary place—very dark, and the smell was dreadful. Diamond stood still for a few moments. He could not see but now he could hear the moaning plainly enough. When he got used to the darkness he discovered his friend lying with her eyes closed in one corner of the room on a bed of little more than rags. He went up and spoke to her, but she made him no answer. She was not even aware that he was there. Diamond saw that she was so sick he could do nothing for her without help. So he took a lump of barley sugar from his pocket, which he had bought for her as he came, and laid it beside her. He then left, having already made up his mind to go and see the tall gentleman, Mr. Raymond, and ask him to do something for Sal's Nanny, as the girl was called.

By the time he got up the steps, three or four women who had seen him go down were standing together at the top waiting for him. They wanted to steal his clothes for their own children, but they had not followed him down for fear Sal might find them there. The moment he appeared they took hold of him and all began talking at once. He told them quite plainly that he had come to see what was the matter with Nanny.

"What do you know about Nanny?" said one of them fiercely. "Wait till old Sal comes home, and you'll catch it for sneaking into her house when she's gone. If you don't give me your jacket, I'll go and fetch her."

"I can't give you my jacket," said Diamond. "It belongs to my father and mother. It's not mine to give. You would not think it right to give away what wasn't yours—would you now?"

"Give it away! No, that I wouldn't. I'd keep it," she said with a rough laugh. "But if the jacket ain't yours, what right have you to keep it? Here, Cherry," she said to one of the others, "make haste. It'll be one go apiece."

They all began to tug at the jacket while Diamond bent down and tried to resist them. But just then they all scampered away, and looking up Diamond saw the tall policeman coming toward him.

"You should have let me come with you, little man," he said, looking down into Diamond's face.

"They've done me no harm," returned Diamond. "Thank you."

"They would have if I hadn't been nearby, though."

"Yes, but you were nearby, you know, so they couldn't."

They walked away together, Diamond telling his new friend how sick poor Nanny was and that he was going to let the tall gentleman know. The policeman guided him the nearest way back to Bloomsbury, and walking fast, Diamond reached Mr. Raymond's door in less than an hour. When he asked if the man was at home, the servant asked what he wanted.

"I want to tell him something."

"But I can't go trouble him with such a message as that."

"He told me to come to him—that is when I could read—and I can."

"How am I to know that?"

Diamond stared with astonishment for one moment, then answered, "Why, I've just told you. That's how you know it."

But this man was made of coarser grain than the policeman, and, instead of seeing from his face that Diamond could not tell a lie, he thought his answer was disrespectful and said, "Do you think I'm going to take your word for it?" and then shut the door in his face.

Diamond turned and sat down on the doorstep, thinking that the tall gentleman must either come in or come out eventually, and that this was certainly the best place to wait in order to see him. He had not waited long before the door opened again, but when he turned around, it was only the servant.

"Get away," he said. "What are you doing on the doorstep?"

"I'm waiting for Mr. Raymond," answered Diamond.

"He's not at home."

"Then I'll wait till he comes," returned Diamond with a smile.

What the man would have done next I do not know, but a step sounded from the hall behind him, and when Diamond looked around again, there was the tall gentleman.

"Who's this, John?" he asked.

"I don't know, sir. An impudent little boy who insists on sitting on the doorstep."

"Please, sir," said Diamond, getting up, "he told me you weren't at home so I sat down to wait for you."

"What!" said Mr. Raymond. "John, this won't do! Is it a habit of yours to turn away my visitors? There'll be someone else to turn away, I'm afraid, if I find any more of this kind of thing. Come in, my little man, I suppose you've come to claim your sixpence."

"No, sir, not that."

"Can't you read yet?"

"Yes, I can now, a little. But I'll come for that next time. I came to tell you about Sal's Nanny."

"Who's Sal's Nanny?"

"The girl at the crossing you talked to the same day I saw you."

"Oh yes, I remember. What's the matter? Has she got run over?"

Then Diamond told him everything.

Now, Mr. Raymond was one of the kindest men in London. He sent at once to have the horse and carriage brought around, took Diamond with him, and drove to the Children's Hospital. There he was well known to everybody, for he was not only a contributor, but he used to go and tell the children stories some afternoons. One of the doctors promised to go find Nanny and do what could be done for her—have her brought to the hospital if possible.

That same night they sent a carriage for her. Old Sal did not object since the girl could be of no use to her sick in bed. So the girl was soon lying in the hospital, for the first time in her life in a nice clean bed. But she knew nothing of the whole affair. She was too sick to know anything.

# CHAPTER SEVENTEEN

# THE EARLY BIRD

Mr. Raymond took Diamond home with him, stopping at the mews to tell his mother that he would send him back soon. Diamond ran in with the message himself, and when he reappeared he had in his hand the torn and crumpled book which North Wind had given him.

"Ah," said Mr. Raymond, "I see you are going to claim your sixpence now."

"I wasn't thinking of that so much," said Diamond. "There's a rhyme in this book I can't quite understand. I want you to tell me what it means, if you please."

"I will if I can," answered Mr. Raymond. "You shall read it to me when we get home, and then I shall see."

With a good many blunders, Diamond read it after a fashion. Mr. Raymond took the little book and read it over again.

Now Mr. Raymond was a poet himself, and so, although he had never been to the back of the north wind, he was able to understand the poem pretty well. But before saying anything about it, he read it over aloud, and Diamond thought he understood it much better already.

"I'll tell you what I think it means," he then said. "It means that people may have their way for a while, if they like, but it will get them into such troubles they'll wish they hadn't had it."

"I know, I know!" said Diamond. "Like the poor cabman next door. He drinks too much."

"Just so," returned Mr. Raymond. "But when people want to do right, things about them will try to help them."

A good deal more talk followed, and Mr. Raymond gave Diamond his sixpence.

"What will you do with it?" he asked.

"Take it home to my mother," he answered. "She has a black teapot with a broken spout, and she keeps all her money in it. It isn't much, but she saves it up to buy shoes for me. And there's baby growing so fast, and he'll want shoes soon. And every sixpence is something, isn't it, sir?"

"To be sure, my man. I hope you'll always make as good use of your money."

"I hope so, sir," replied Diamond.

"And here's a book for you, full of pictures and stories and poems. I wrote it myself for the children at the hospital where Nanny is."

"I make songs myself. They're awfully silly, but they please baby, and that's all they're meant for."

"Couldn't you let me hear one of them now?" said Mr. Raymond.

"No, sir, I couldn't. I forget them as soon as I've done with them. Besides, I couldn't make a line without baby on my knee. We make them together, you know."

"I suspect the child's a genius," said the poet to himself, "and that's what makes people think him silly."

If any of you child readers want to know what a genius is, I will give you this very short answer: It means someone who understands things without anybody else telling him what they mean. God makes a few such now and then to teach the rest of us.

"Do you like riddles?" asked Mr. Raymond, turning over the pages of his own book.

"I don't know what a riddle is," replied Diamond.

"It's something that means something else, and you've got to find out what the something else is."

Mr. Raymond read one out of the book he had written.

> I have only one foot, but thousands of toes;
> My one foot stands, but never goes.
> I have many arms, and they're mighty all;
> And hundreds of fingers, large and small.
> From the ends of my fingers my beauty grows.
> I breathe with my hair, and I drink with my toes.
> I grow bigger and bigger about the waist,
> And yet I am always very tight laced.
> None ever saw me eat—I've no mouth to bite;
> Yet I eat all day in the full sunlight.
> In the summer with song I shake and quiver,
> But in winter I fast and groan and shiver.

"Do you know what that means, Diamond?" he asked when he had finished.

"No, indeed, I do not," answered Diamond.

"Then you can read it for yourself, and think it over," said Mr. Raymond, giving him the book. "And now you had better go home to your mother. When you've found the answer to the riddle, you can come again."

If you are thinking that Diamond could not have been a genius if he could not understand the riddle, I will answer you by saying that a genius finds out truths, not tricks. And if you do not understand that, I am afraid you must be content to wait till you grow older and know more.

When Diamond got home he found his father already through for the day, sitting by the fire and looking rather miserable, for he had a headache and felt sick.

The next day he had to stay in bed and by the next day he was very sick indeed.

Long before the father got well, the mother's savings were all but gone. She did not say a word about it to him, and one night, when she could not help crying, she came into Diamond's room so that his father wouldn't hear her. When the boy heard her sobbing, he was frightened, and said:

"Is Father worse, Mother?"

"No, Diamond," she answered, "he's getting better."

"Then why are you crying, Mother?"

"Because my money is almost all gone," she replied.

"That makes me think of a little poem baby and I learned out of North Wind's book today, the one about the early bird catching the worm."

"I wish you were like that little bird in the story, Diamond, and could catch worms for yourself," said his mother as she rose to go and look after her husband.

Diamond lay awake for a few minutes, thinking what he could do to catch worms. It was very little trouble to make up his mind, however, and still less to go to sleep after it.

He got up in the morning as soon as he heard the men moving in the yard. He tucked in his little brother so that he could not tumble out of bed, and then went out, leaving the door open so that if he cried his mother would hear him at once. When Diamond got into the yard he found the stable door just opened.

"I'm the early bird, I think," he said to himself. "I hope I shall catch the worm."

He would not ask for any help, fearing that someone might disapprove of his project and make him stop. With great difficulty, but with the help of a broken chair he brought down from his bedroom, he managed to put the harness on Diamond. If the old horse had the least objection to the proceeding, of course, the boy could not have done it. But even when it came to the bridle, the horse opened his mouth for the bit, just as if he had been taking the apple which Diamond sometimes gave him. He fastened the cheek-strap very carefully, just in the usual hole, for fear of choking his friend, or else letting the bit get among his teeth. It was a job to get the saddle on, but with the chair he managed it. The collar was almost the worst part of the business, but there Diamond could help Diamond. He held his head very low till his little master had got it over and turned it round, and then he lifted his head and shook the collar on to his shoulders. The yoke was rather difficult, but when Diamond had laid the traces over the horse's neck, the weight was not too much for the young master. He got it right at last, and led the horse out of the stable.

By this time there were several of the men watching him, but they would not interfere, they were so anxious to see how he would get over the various difficulties. They followed him as far as the stable door, and there stood watching him again as he put the horse between the shafts, got them up one after another into the loops, fastened the traces, the belly band, the breeching, and the reins.

Then he got his whip. The moment he mounted the box, the men broke into a hearty cheer of delight at his success. But they would not let him go without a general inspection of the harness, and although they found everything just right, they never allowed him to do it for himself again the whole time his father was ill.

The cheer brought his mother to the window, and there she saw her little boy setting out alone with the cab in the gray of morning. She tugged at the window, but it was stiff, and before she could open it, Diamond was out of the mews and was already a good way down the street. "Diamond, Diamond!" she called, but there was no answer except from Jack.

"Never fear for him, ma'am," he said. "It 'ud be only a devil as would hurt him, an' there ain't so many o' them as some folk 'ud have you believe."

"But he won't upset the cab, will he, Jack?"

"Not he, ma'am. At least he's as little likely to do it as the oldest man in the stable. How's the gov'nor today, ma'am?"

"A good deal better, thank you," she answered, then closed the window.

Diamond had resolved to go straight to the cab stand where he was best known, but before he got across Oxford Street he was hailed by a man who wanted to catch a train and was in too great a hurry to think about the driver. Having carried him to King's Cross in good time, and receiving a good fare in return, Diamond set off again in great spirits and reached the stand in safety. He was first there even with the delay of his detour to King's Cross.

As the men arrived they all greeted him kindly and asked about his father.

"Ain't you afraid of the old horse running away with you?" asked one.

"He wouldn't run away with me," answered Diamond. "He knows I'm only getting the shillings for Father. Or if he did he would only run home."

"Well, you're a plucky one," said the man. "I wish ye luck."

"Thank you, sir," replied Diamond.

In the course of the day one man did try to cut in front of Diamond, but he was a stranger, and the shout from the rest of the cabmen let him see that it would not do.

Once a policeman came up and asked him for his number. Diamond showed his father's badge and said with a smile:

"Father's sick at home, and so I came out with the cab. But I can drive. And besides, the old horse could go alone if he had to."

"Just as well, I daresay. You're a pair of 'em. But you *are* a rum 'un for a cabby—ain't you now?" said the policeman.

In a few minutes a gentleman hailed him. "Are you the driver of this cab?" he asked.

"Yes, sir," said Diamond, showing his badge, which he was very proud of.

"You're the youngest cabman I ever saw. How am I to know you won't break all my bones?"

"I would rather break all my own," answered Diamond. "But if you're afraid, never mind me. I will soon get another fare."

"I'll risk it," said the gentleman, and opening the door himself he jumped in. He was going a good distance and soon found that Diamond got him over the ground well enough.

Diamond had been thinking about the riddle Mr. Raymond had told him, and this gentleman looked rather smart. Diamond had thought of the answer himself but didn't think it could be right, so when he reached the end of his journey, he got down very quickly, and with his head just looking in at the window as the gentleman was gathering his gloves and newspapers, said:

"Please, sir, can you tell me the meaning of a riddle?"

"You must tell me the riddle first," answered the gentleman, amused. Diamond repeated the riddle.

"That's easy enough," he said. "It's a tree."

"But then how can it eat all day long?"

"It sucks in its food through the tiniest holes in its leaves," he answered. "Its breath is its food. And it can't do it except in the daylight."

"Thank you, sir, thank you," returned Diamond. "I'm only sorry I couldn't find it out myself. Mr. Raymond would have liked that better."

"You don't need to tell him anyone told you."

Diamond gave him a stare which came from the very back of the north wind, where that kind of thing is unknown.

"That would be cheating," he said at last.

"Aren't you a cabby?"

"Cabbies don't cheat."

"Oh, they don't?"

"I'm sure my father doesn't."

"What's your fare then, young man?"

"Well, I think the distance is three miles—so that would be two shillings. But Father says sixpence a mile is too little, though we can't ask for more."

"I think you're wrong. It's over four miles. So here's three shillings. Will that do?"

"Thank you kindly, sir. I'll tell my father how good you were to me—first to tell me the riddle, and then to put me right about the distance and give me sixpence extra. I'm sure it will help him get well."

When Diamond went home that night, he carried with him one pound, one shilling, and sixpence, and a few coppers extra. His mother had been very anxious indeed, but when he at last drew up, with the old horse and cab looking all right, there sat Diamond in the box, his pale face looking triumphant as a full moon in the twilight.

When he drew up at the stable door, Jack came out and after a good many questions and congratulations, said:

"You go in to your mother, Diamond. I'll put up the old horse. I'll take good care of him. He do deserve some attention, he do."

"Thank you, Jack," said Diamond, who bounded into the house and into the arms of his mother, who was waiting for him at the top of the stair. The poor anxious woman led him into his own room, sat down on his bed, took him on her lap as if he had been a baby, and cried.

"How's Father?" asked Diamond, almost afraid to ask.

"Better, my child," she answered, "but uneasy about you, my dear."

"Didn't you tell him I was the early bird gone out to catch the worm?"

"So that was what put this into your head."

"And here's my worm," he said.

If only you could have seen her face as he poured the shillings and sixpences and pence into her lap! She burst out crying a second time, and ran with the money to her husband.

And how pleased he was! It did him no end of good. But while he was counting the coins, Diamond turned to baby, who was lying awake in his cradle, and took him up, saying:

"Baby, baby! I haven't seen you for a whole year."

And then he began to sing to him a rhyme out of Mr. Raymond's book.

# Chapter Eighteen

# Diamond Takes a Fare the Wrong Way Right

"Oh, Mother," said Diamond after he had finished singing to baby, "just think if Father had been a poor man and hadn't had a cab and old Diamond! What should I have done?"

"We should have all starved, my precious Diamond," said his mother, whose pride in her boy was even greater than her joy in the shillings. Both of them together made her heart ache, for pleasure can do that as well as pain.

"Oh no, we wouldn't have," said Diamond. "I could have taken Nanny's crossing till she came back, and then the money, instead of going for Old Sal's gin, would have gone for Father's beef tea. I wonder what Nanny will do when she gets well again. Somebody else will have taken her crossing by that time. I wonder what the angels do—when they're extra happy, you know—when they've been driving cabs all day and taking home the money to their mothers. Do you think they ever sing nonsense, Mother?"

"I daresay they've got their own sort of it," answered his

mother. Actually, she was thinking more of her twenty-one shillings and sixpence, and of the nice dinner she would get for her sick husband the next day, than of angels and their nonsense, when she said it. But Diamond found her answer all right.

"But it must be very pretty nonsense," said Diamond, "and not like that silly 'hey diddle, the cat and the fiddle'!"

Diamond chattered away. Whatever rose in his happy little heart ran out of his mouth, and did his father and mother good. When he went to bed, which he did early for he was tired, he was still thinking what the nonsense could be like which the angels sang when they were too happy to sing sense. But before coming to any conclusion he fell fast asleep. And no wonder, for it was a very difficult question!

The next morning Diamond was up almost as early as before. This time he made no secret of what he was about. By the time he reached the stable, several of the men were there. They asked him a good many questions as to his luck the day before and he told them all they wanted to know. But when he began to harness the old horse again, they pushed him aside and began to do it all for him. So Diamond ran in and had another few bites of bread and butter. And even though he had never been so tired as he was the night before, he started out quite fresh this morning. It was a cloudy day, and the wind was blowing hard from the north—so hard that sometimes Diamond wished he had a strap to fasten himself down with to keep him from being blown right off the box. But he did not really mind it.

There was not much business doing. And Diamond was cold even though his mother had bundled him up as warmly as she could. But he was too well aware of his dignity to get inside his cab as some did. A cabman ought to be above minding the weather—at least so Diamond thought. Before long he was called to a nearby house where a young woman with a heavy box wanted to be taken to the shipyards to catch a steamer for the coast.

He did not find it at all pleasant going so near the river, for there were many ruffians about. However, he reached the wharf and set down his passenger without any problem. But as he turned to go back, some men about began calling him names and then began trying to steal the money the young woman had given him. They were just pulling him down off his cab, and Diamond was shouting for the police, when a pale-faced man in very shabby clothes, but with the look of a gentleman somewhere about him, came up and drove them off with his stick.

"Now, my little man," he said, "get away while you can. Don't lose any time. This is not a good place for you."

But Diamond was not in the habit of thinking only of himself. He saw that his new friend looked weary, if not sick, and very poor.

"Won't you jump in, sir?" he said, "I will take you wherever you like."

"Thank you, my man, but I have no money, so I can't."

"Oh! I don't want any money. I shall be much happier if you will get in. You have saved me from those men. I owe you a lift, sir."

"Which way are you going?"

"To Charing Cross. But I don't mind where I go."

"Well, I am very tired. If you will take me to Charing Cross, I shall be greatly obliged to you. I have walked from Gravesend and have hardly a penny left."

He opened the door and got in, and Diamond drove away. As he drove, he could not help thinking he had seen the gentleman—for Diamond knew he was a gentleman—before. But he could not remember where or when. In the meantime, the man had been thinking, and after a few moments called out to Diamond, who stopped his horse, got down, and went to the window to see what the man wanted.

"If you don't mind taking me to Chiswick, I would be able to pay you when we got there. It's a long way, but I could pay you the whole fare."

"Very well, sir," said Diamond. "I shall be happy to."

He was just clambering up again when the gentleman put his head out of the window and said:

"It's Mr. Coleman's place; but I'll direct you when we come into the neighborhood."

Suddenly it flashed upon Diamond's mind who he was. But

he got up on the box to continue on and arrange his thoughts before saying anything further.

The gentleman was Mr. Evans, to whom Miss Coleman was to have been married, and Diamond had seen him several times with her in the garden. I have said that he had not behaved very well to Miss Coleman. Evans had put off their marriage more than once because he had been somewhat of a coward. He had been taken in by Mr. Coleman as a junior partner in Coleman's business, and it was partially Mr. Evan's fault that Mr. Coleman had made the investments that had ruined his business. The ship which North Wind had sunk had been their last venture and Mr. Evans had been on board. He was one of those in the single boatload which had managed to reach a desert island, and he had gone through many hardships and sufferings since then. But his troubles had done him no end of good, for they had made him begin to think, and he had come to see that he had been foolish as well as unkind to Miss Coleman. Before he got home again he had even begun to understand that no man can be in a hurry to become rich without going against the will of God, in which case it is a frightful thing to be successful. So he had come back a more humble man and longing to ask Miss Coleman to forgive him. But he had no idea what ruin had fallen upon the Colemans. Hence, he never doubted that he would find everything just as it was when he had left, and thus directed Diamond to their old home, which now belonged to someone else. But if he had not come upon Diamond, he would never have thought of going there first.

Diamond had heard his father and mother making some remarks concerning Mr. Evans that had made the boy doubtful of him. What was he to do now? He knew it was of no use to drive Mr. Evans to Chiswick. So he went rather slowly until he could make up his mind what to do. If he told him what had happened to the Colemans, the man might put off going to see them, and Diamond was certain that Miss Coleman, at least, must want very much to see Mr. Evans. He was pretty sure also that the best thing in any case was to bring them together and let them set matters right for themselves.

The moment he came to this conclusion, he changed his

course from westward to northward, and went straight for Mr. Coleman's poor little house in Hoxton. Mr. Evans was too tired and much too occupied with his thoughts to take the least notice of the streets they passed through and had no suspicion, therefore, of the change of direction.

By this time the wind had increased almost to a hurricane, and before they reached the street where Mr. Coleman lived, the stormy gale blew so tremendously that when Miss Coleman opened the door to go for a walk, it dashed against the wall with such a bang that she went in again. Five minutes later, Diamond drew up at the door. As soon as he had entered the street, however, the wind blew right behind them, and he had so much difficulty to stop the cab against it that one of the reins broke. Diamond jumped off his box, knocked loudly at the house door, then turned to the cab and said—before Mr. Evans had even begun to think something must be amiss:

"Please, sir, my harness has given way. Would you mind stepping in here for a few minutes? They're friends of mine. I'll take you where you like after I've got it mended. I won't be long."

Tired and hungry, Mr. Evans took the boy's suggestion and walked in at the door which the maid held open with difficulty against the wind. She took Mr. Evans for a visitor, as indeed he was, and showed him into the room on the ground floor. Diamond, who had followed into the hall, whispered to her as she closed the door.

"Tell Miss Coleman. It's Miss Coleman he wants to see."

"I don't know," said the maid. "He don't look much like a gentleman."

"He is though, and I know him, and so does Miss Coleman."

The maid remembered Diamond, having seen him when he and his father brought the ladies home. So she believed him and went to do what he told her.

What went on in the little parlor when Miss Coleman came down does not belong to my story, which is all about Diamond. If he had known that Miss Coleman thought that Mr. Evans was dead, perhaps he would have done it differently. There was a cry and a running to and fro in the house, and then all was quiet again.

Almost as soon as Mr. Evans went in, the wind began to cease, and was now still. Diamond found that by making the strap just a little tighter than was quite comfortable for the old horse, he could do very well for the time being. Thinking it better to let him have his bag of oats in this quiet place, he sat on the box till old Diamond could eat his dinner. In a little while Mr. Evans came out and asked him to come in. Diamond obeyed, and to his delight Miss Coleman put her arms around him and kissed him. And that was payment enough! not to mention the five precious shillings she gave him, which he could not refuse because his mother wanted them so much at home for his father. He left almost as happy as they were themselves.

The rest of the day he did better, and what a story he had to tell his father and mother about his adventures when he went home. They asked him so many questions. Some of them he could answer, some he could not. And his father seemed so much better from seeing that his boy was already not only useful to his own family but to other people as well, and already learning to judge what was wise and able to do work that was worth doing.

For two weeks Diamond kept on driving his cab and keeping his family. He had begun to be known about some parts of London, and people prefered taking his cab because they liked what they heard of him. One gentleman who lived near the mews hired him to carry him into the city every morning at a certain hour; and Diamond was punctual as clockwork. That took some doing because his father's watch was not much to be depended on and he had also to watch the big clock of St. George's Church. But between the two, however, he did make a success of it.

After those two weeks, his father was able to go out again. Then Diamond went to ask about Nanny, and this led to something else.

# Chapter Nineteen

# Little Daylight

The first day his father resumed work, Diamond went with him as usual. In the afternoon, however, his father went home and Diamond drove the cab the rest of the day. It was hard for old Diamond to do all the work, but they could not afford another horse. However, they fed him well, and he did bravely,

The next morning his father was so much stronger that Diamond thought he might go and ask Mr. Raymond to take him to see Nanny. He found him at home. Mr. Raymond received him with his usual kindness, agreed at once, and walked with him to the hospital, which was nearby. It was an old-fashioned place, a home for poor sick children, who were carefully tended for love's sake.

When Diamond followed Mr. Raymond into the room where the children lay who were recovering from their illnesses, he saw a number of little iron bedsteads with their heads to the walls, and in every one of them lay a child whose face was a story in itself. In some, health had begun to appear upon the cheeks, and the hints of coming springtime shone in their eyes. In others there were more of the signs of winter still left. Their faces reminded one of snow and keen cutting winds, rather than of sunshine and soft breezes and butterflies. But even in them the suffering was less than it had been.

Diamond looked all around but could see no Nanny. "Nanny's not here," he said to Mr. Raymond.

"Oh yes she is, right over there. He pointed to a bed near where Diamond was standing.

"That's not Nanny," he said.

"It is Nanny. Illness sometimes makes a great difference on a face."

*Why, that girl must have been to the back of the north wind!* thought Diamond, but he said nothing, only stared at her. And as he stared, something of the old Nanny began to dawn through the face of the new Nanny. The old Nanny, though a friendly girl, had been rough, blunt in her speech, and dirty. But now she was sweet and gentle. And Diamond could not help thinking of words which he had heard in the church the day before: "Surely it is good to be afflicted," or something like that. North Wind, somehow or other, must have had to do with her. She had grown from a rough girl into a gentle maiden.

Mr. Raymond, however, was not surprised, for he was used to seeing such lovely changes on the children that came here—something like the change which comes on the crawling, many-footed caterpillar when it turns sick and changes into a butterfly, with two wings instead of feet. Nanny's whole face had grown so refined and sweet that Diamond did not recognize her. But as he gazed, the best of the old face, all the true and good part of it—that which was Nanny herself—dawned upon him and he saw for himself that it was indeed Nanny—very worn, but grown beautiful,

He went up to her. She smiled. He had heard her laugh, but had never seen her smile before.

"Nanny, do you know me?" asked Diamond.

She only smiled again as if the question was amusing.

She was not likely to forget him. Although she did not yet know it was he who had gotten her there, he was the only boy except Jim who had ever shown her kindness.

In the meantime Mr. Raymond was going from bed to bed, talking to all the children. Everyone knew him and everyone was eager to have a look and a smile and a kind word from him.

Diamond sat down on a stool at the head of Nanny's bed. She laid her hand in his. He was the first visitor she had.

Suddenly a little voice called out:

"Won't Mr. Raymond tell us a story?"

"Oh yes, please do! Please do!" cried several little voices. For Mr. Raymond was in the habit of telling them a story when he came, and they enjoyed it far more than the other nice things he gave them.

"Very well," said Mr. Raymond. "What sort of a story shall it be?"

"A true story," said one little girl.

"A fairy tale," said a little boy.

"Well," said Mr. Raymond, "I suppose I must choose. And since I can't think of any true stories just now, I will tell you a fairy one."

"Oh jolly!"

"It came into my head this morning as I got out of bed," continued Mr. Raymond.

"Then nobody has ever heard it before?" asked one older girl.

"No, nobody."

"Oh!" exclaimed several, thinking it very special to have the first hearing of a new story.

Mr. Raymond stood in the middle of the room, while the children prepared themselves, turned their heads to hear him better, and uttered many feeble exclamations of expected pleasure. Diamond kept his place by Nanny's side, with her hand in his. Everyone listened with satisfaction and great attention. They all liked it so well that Mr. Raymond wrote it down later and put it in a book with his other stories. And here is the story he told them:

Near every palace there must be a wood, and the nearer the better, though not all the way around it. And there was a very grand wood indeed beside the palace of the king who was going to be Daylight's father. Near the house this wood was kept neat and trim, but gradually it got wilder and denser the farther from the palace it went, and some people said it even had wild beasts in it some distance away.

One glorious summer morning little Daylight was born. She

was a beautiful baby, with such bright eyes that she might have come right from the sun. But she was such a lively baby that she might just as well have come out of the wind. There was great happiness all about the palace, for this was the queen's first baby.

But there is one disadvantage of living near a wood: you do not always know who your neighbors might be. Everybody knew there were several fairies living in this wood within a few miles of the palace. And they always had something to do with every new baby that came. For fairies live so much longer than we do that they can have business with many generations of human mortals. The curious houses they lived in were very well known—one, a hollow oak, a birch tree; another, a hut of intertwined growing trees patched up with moss. But there was another fairy who had come to the place only recently. She was a wicked old thing and always tried to be mean whenever she had the chance. She lived in a mud house in a swampy part of the forest.

Fairies always came out at the christening of new babies, especially after the birth of princes or princesses, to bestow their remarkable gifts. So it is not hard to explain why wicked fairies should choose the same time to do unkind things. But I do not know of any interference on the part of a wicked fairy that did not turn out a good thing in the end. What a good thing, for instance, it was that one princess should sleep for a hundred years! For she was saved from all the young men who would have wanted to marry her but who were not worthy of her. And she came awake at exactly the right moment when just the right prince kissed her. I think a good many girls would be far better off to sleep until the same fate overtook them.

Of course all the known fairies were invited to little Daylight's christening. But the old wicked hag was there without being asked. The good fairies could not make her powerless, nor could they block her tricks by their own gifts ahead of time, for they could not tell what she might try to do.

Five fairies had one after the other given the child such gifts as they thought best, and the fifth had just stepped back to her place when, mumbling a laugh between her toothless gums, the wicked fairy hobbled out into the middle of the circle and said:

"Please, Your Grace, I'm very deaf. Would Your Grace mind repeating the princess's name."

"Of course," said the archbishop. "The child's name is little Daylight."

"And little daylight it shall be!" cried the fairy, "and little good shall any of her gifts do her. For I bestow on her the gift of sleeping all day long, whether she wants to or not. Ha, ha! He, he! Hi, hi!"

Then out stepped the sixth fairy, who, of course, the others had arranged should come after the wicked one, in order to undo as much as she might.

"If she must sleep all day," she said, "she shall at least stay awake all night."

*Not such a nice thought for her mother and me!* thought the poor king. For they loved her too much to turn her over to nurses, as most kings and queens do—and are sorry for it afterward.

"You spoke before I was done," said the wicked fairy. "That's against the law. It gives me another chance. I wasn't through laughing. I had only got to Hi, hi! and I had yet to go all through Ho, ho! and Hu, hu! So I decree that if she stays awake all night, her spirits shall come and go with the moon. Ho, ho! Hu, hu!"

But out stepped another fairy, for they had been wise enough to keep two in reserve, because they knew the wicked fairy would try every trick she could think of.

"Until," said the seventh good fairy, "a prince comes who shall kiss her without knowing it."

The wicked fairy made a horrible noise like an angry cat, for she could see that she had been outsmarted, and she hobbled away. She could not pretend that she had not finished her speech this time, for she had laughed Ho, ho! and Hu, hu!

When the assembly broke up, everyone was miserable, and the king and queen prepared for a good many sleepless nights, and the lady at the head of the nursery department was anything but comfortable with the prospects of what lay before her.

I will not attempt to describe what life was like in the palace. At certain seasons the halls rang all night with bursts of laughter from little Daylight. But she always dropped off to sleep at the first hint of dawn in the east. When the moon was full she was in glorious spirits. But as the moon got smaller, she faded too, until at last she became pale and withered like a poor, sickly child. At such times the night was as quiet as the day, for the poor little baby lay in her cradle both night and day with hardly a motion or a sound. But then as the moon again began to grow, her spirits would begin to revive. She would grow better and better until for a few short days, when the moon was big, she was splendidly well. And when she was well she was always her merriest when out in the moonlight.

As she grew older she became such a favorite that there were always some who would arrange to stay awake at night to be with her. But she soon began to take every chance to get away from her nurses to go out and enjoy the moonlight alone. Her father and mother had by this time gotten so used to the odd state of things that they no longer wondered at them. And thus things went on until she was nearly seventeen years of age.

As she grew older she grew more and more beautiful, with the sunniest hair and the loveliest eyes of heavenly blue. But so much more painful and sad was the change as her bad time came. The more beautiful she was in the full moon, the more withered and worn she became as the moon waned. By and by, when the moon was small, she took on the look of an old woman, exhausted with suffering, thin and stooped as if she were eighty years old. She did not like to be seen or touched by anyone else during this season and had to be put to bed to await the new flow of life.

A little way from the palace there was a great open meadow, covered with the greenest and softest grass. This was her favorite place, for here the moon shone free and glorious. She had an old-fashioned little house built for her here and no one could go there without her permission. She often wandered into the woods every night when the moon was shrinking, and sometimes fell asleep in the forest far from her house. But the good fairies watched over her and always managed to get her back to her cottage before she was lost altogether.

About this time in a neighboring kingdom there was a great uprising after the death of the old king; and his son, the young prince, was forced to flee for his life, disguised like a peasant.

He had little food or money, and suffered much from hunger and tiredness.

He had been walking for a day or two through the wood near the palace of Daylight's father and had practically nothing to eat, when he came upon the strangest little house, where lived a nice motherly old woman. This was one of the good fairies. The moment she saw him she knew quite well who he was. She received him with kindness and gave him bread and milk, which he thought the most delicious food he had ever tasted. She asked him to stay the night, and when he awoke the next morning he was amazed to find how well and strong he felt. As he left she begged him to come back if he found himself continuing in the neighborhood. She stood at the door of her little house looking after him as he disappeared through all the trees. Then she said, "I am glad he has come at last!" and went in.

The prince wandered and wandered and got nowhere. What part the good fairies had in making him lose his way I can't say. But the sun sank and sank and went out of sight, and he seemed no nearer the end of the wood than ever. He sat down on a fallen tree and ate a bit of the bread the old woman had given him. Before long the moon began to come up very slowly. It was of good size and nearly fully round. Feeling better after his piece of bread, he got up and walked on, but he knew not where.

After walking a long distance he thought he was coming out of the forest, but when he reached what he thought was the last of it, he found himself only on the edge of a great open meadow in the middle of it, all covered with grass. The moon was shining very bright and he thought he had never seen a more lovely spot. Still he was lonely and it looked a bit dreary. He sat down again but because it was night he was unable to see the house at the other side of the glade.

All at once he saw something in the middle of the grass. What could it be? It moved, then came nearer. It was a girl all dressed in white, gleaming in the moonlight. Nearer and nearer she came. It must be some strange creature of the wood. But when she came nearer he could no longer doubt that she was a human girl—she had sunny hair, clear blue eyes, and the loveliest face he had ever seen. All at once she began singing like a nightingale, and dancing all about the meadow, all the while looking at the moon.

She passed close to where he stood watching, behind a tree, singing and dancing and waving her arms over her head. Then, as if tired, she threw herself on the grass and lay gazing at the moon. The prince was almost afraid to breathe for fear of startling her, and stood still, watching her, for over an hour. He dreamed of coming here every night the moon was out to see her again, for to have found such a beautiful spirit of the wood as this was far better than the kingdom he had left behind. But while he dreamed like this, all at once she sprang to her feet and began singing again in her entrancing voice. She looked even more beautiful than ever. Again she began dancing, and danced away into the distance. The prince watched as eagerly as before, but eventually fell asleep.

When he awoke it was broad daylight and the princess was nowhere to be seen.

He could not leave the place. What if she should come the next night! He had to see her again, no matter how hungry he got from the waiting. He walked around the meadow to see if he could discover her footprints. But the grass was so short and her steps had been so light that she had not left a single trace behind her. He walked halfway around the wood and then spotted a lovely little house, with thatched roof and low eaves, surrounded by a beautiful garden with doves and peacocks walking in it. Could this be where she lived?

Forgetting his appearance, he walked to the door, knocked, and asked for a piece of bread. The good-natured cook asked him in and gave him an excellent breakfast instead. He asked many questions but was able to learn nothing about the princess, because the cook did not want to talk about her mistress to a peasant lad who came to the door begging for his breakfast.

As he rose to leave, he remembered the old woman's cottage and asked the cook if she knew anything of such a place. She said she knew it well enough, adding with a smile, "If you're going there, mind what you are about."

"Why do you say that?"

"Because if you're up to any mischief, she'll make you repent of it."

"That seems to be the best thing that could happen under the circumstances," answered the prince.

"Well, you're probably right," said the cook, and gave him instructions how to get there.

However, the prince remained in the forest all that day, waiting anxiously for the night in the hope that the princess would appear again. And he was not disappointed, for as soon as the moon was up she came again—not dressed in white as before, but this time in a pale blue. She danced and sang again, always moving in large circles about the meadow, and the prince watched, entranced with her loveliness. All night long he watched her, but he did not dare go near her or speak to her. And as the moon gradually went down she retreated from sight until he could see her no longer.

Weary as he was he set out for the old woman's cottage where he had spent his first night in the forest. He arrived just in time for breakfast, which she shared with him. Then he went to bed and slept for many hours. When he awoke the sun was already going down and he set off in a great hurry. But he lost his way and was not able to find the path back to the meadow. The moon was high in the sky before he reached the glade. But then he was happy again, for there was the princess again, dancing in a dress that shone like gold. He thought she was even more beautiful than before. He watched, and as she danced the wind rose and clouds began to gather about the moon. The trees moaned and the prince feared the princess would go in because of the coming storm. But she went on dancing more joyously than ever, her golden dress and sunny hair streaming out in the wind and her arms waving toward the moon.

By this time there were growlings of distant thunder. Just as she passed the tree where he stood, a flash of lightning blinded him for a moment, and when he could see again, to his horror, the princess lay on the ground. He ran to her, thinking she had been struck by the lightning. But when she heard him coming, she sprang back to her feet.

"What do you want?" she asked.

"I beg your pardon. I thought—the lightning . . ." said the prince, hesitating.

"There is nothing the matter," said the princess.

"I'm sorry," said the prince, and turned to go.

"Come back," said the princess.

He obeyed, turned, and stood before her.

"Can you tell me what the sun is like?" she asked.

"What's the good of asking something you already know?"

"But I don't know," she answered.

"Everybody knows what the sun is like."

"But I'm not everybody. I've never seen the sun."

"Then you can't know what it's like till you do see it."

"I think you must be a prince," said the princess.

"Do I look like one?" asked the prince.

"I can't quite say that."

"Then why do you think so?"

"Because you both *do* what you are told and *speak* the truth.—Is the sun so very bright?"

"As bright as the lightning."

"But it doesn't go out like that, does it?"

"Oh no. It shines like the moon and sets like the moon, and is the same shape as the moon, only so bright that you can't even look at it for a moment."

"But I *would* look at it," said the princess.

"But you couldn't," said the prince.

"But I could," said the princess.

"Why don't you, then?"

"Because I can't."

"Why can't you?"

"Because I can't wake. And I shall never wake until—"

The princess hid her face in her hands, turned away, and walked slowly toward the house. The prince wanted to follow her, but knew he shouldn't. He waited a long time, and at last set off for the old woman's cottage. It was past midnight when he arrived, but to his surprise the old woman was peeling potatoes. Fairies are fond of doing odd things.

"What are you doing up at this time of night?" asked the prince.

"Getting your supper ready, my son," she answered.

"Oh, I don't need any supper," said the prince.

"Ah! you've seen Daylight," she said.

"I've seen a princess who never saw it," said the prince.

"Do you like her?" asked the fairy.

"Oh, more than you can believe."

"A fairy can believe anything," said the old woman.

"Then you are a fairy?" asked the prince.

"Yes," she said. "And I'll tell you a secret: she's a princess."

"Well, I'll tell *you* a secret. I'm a prince."

"I know that."

"How do you know it?"

"By the curl of the third eyelash on your left eyelid."

"Which corner do you count from?"

"That's a secret."

"Another secret? Well, at least if I'm a prince, there can be no harm in telling me about the princess."

"But it's just the princess I can't tell."

And try as he might, the prince could get nothing more out of the fairy about Daylight, and he had to go to bed with his questions unanswered.

Now, wicked fairies are not bound by the law the good fairies obey, and this always seems to give them an advantage. But it doesn't really matter, for what the wicked fairies do never succeeds anyway, and in fact, in the end it brings about the very thing they are trying to prevent. So you see that despite all their cleverness, wicked fairies are actually dreadfully stupid, for, although from the beginning of the world they have really helped instead of thwarting the good fairies, not one of them is a bit wiser for it. So they keep trying to do bad things, even though they can never succeed at it.

Up till now the wicked swamp fairy who had put Daylight under her spell did not even know the prince was in the neighborhood. When she discovered it she put him under a spell that kept him from finding his way back to the meadow. He wandered about the forest all night and then fell fast asleep. The same thing happened for seven days in a row, during which time he could not even find the good fairy's cottage. After the third quarter of the moon, however, the bad fairy thought there was nothing for her to worry about, for there was no chance of a prince wishing to kiss the princess during that time. So on the first day of the fourth quarter of the moon, he did find the cottage, and the next day he found the meadow. For the next week he went to it every night, but the princess never came. And even if she had come, he would not have known her, for during this time she always wore black and looked like a worn and decrepit creature indeed, so different from the glorious Princess Daylight.

At last one night when there was no moon at all, he ventured near the house. He heard voices talking. It was past midnight, but her attendants were very uneasy about the princess because the one whose turn it was to watch her had fallen asleep, and no one knew which way into the wood she had wandered. When the prince understood from what they said that she had disappeared, he plunged at once into the forest to see if he could find her. For hours he roamed, but saw no one.

It was getting toward the dawn when he came to a great birch tree and sat down at the foot of it. While he sat there—very miserable, you may be sure—he heard a moan, which seemed to come from the other side of the tree. He jumped to his feet, ran around, and saw a human form in a little dark heap on the earth. There was just light enough from the coming dawn for him to see that it was not the princess. He lifted the limp body in his arms, hardly heavier than a child, and carried it to a comfortable spot. The face was that of an old woman, but it had a strange look. A black hood concealed her hair, and her eyes were closed. He laid her down as gently as he could, rubbed her hands, and put a few drops into her mouth from a tiny bottle the good fairy had given him. Then he took off his coat and wrapped it about her. In a little while she opened her eyes and looked at him—so sadly! The tears rose and flowed down her gray wrinkled cheeks, but she never said a word. She closed her eyes again, but the tears kept on flowing, and her whole appearance was so utterly pitiful that the prince was near crying too. He begged her to tell him what was the matter, promising to do all he could to help her; but still she did not speak. He thought she was dying, and finally took her in his arms again to carry her to the princess's house, where he thought the good-natured cook might be able to do something to help her. When he lifted her, the tears flowed even faster and she gave such a sad moan that it went right to his heart.

"Mother, Mother!" he said, which is the kind way in which any young man in that country would address a woman who was much older than himself. "Poor mother!" and he kissed her on the withered lips.

She started, and her eyes immediately opened upon him. But he did not see them at first, for it was still very dark, and he was watching his way as he walked through the trees toward the house.

Just as he approached the door she began to move about as they went, and then became so restless in his arms that, unable to carry her a step farther, he decided to lay her down on the grass. But she stood upright on her feet. The hood dropped and her hair fell about her face. The first gleam of the morning shone on her face, a face that was bright as the dawn she had never seen before this day, and her eyes were lovely as the sky of deepest blue.

The prince jumped back in surprise. It was Daylight herself whom he had carried out of the forest! He fell at her feet, hardly daring to look up. She took his hand, kissed it, and then he rose.

"You kissed me when I was an old woman," she said. "Now I kiss you when I am again a young princess."

He gazed into her eyes as she looked with delight upon the spreading dawn. Then she said, "Is that the sun coming?"

# Chapter Twenty

# Ruby

The children were delighted with the story and Mr. Raymond promised to search his brain for another, and when he had found one to bring it to them. Diamond said goodbye to Nanny, promised to come see her again soon, and went away with him.

Now Mr. Raymond had been thinking about what he could do for both Diamond and Nanny. He had met Diamond's father and had been pleased with him. So as they walked away together he began to talk with Diamond.

"Nanny will have to leave the hospital soon, Diamond."

"I'm glad of that, sir."

"But what do you think she will do when they send her out again?"

"I don't know, but I've been thinking about it. Her crossing was taken long ago by someone else. And I couldn't bear to see Nanny fight for it, especially as the boy who sweeps there now is a poor lame fellow. Isn't there anything else she could do, sir?"

"Not without being taught, I'm afraid."

"Well, couldn't somebody teach her something?"

"Couldn't you teach her, Diamond?"

"I don't know anything myself, sir. I *could* teach her to dress the baby, but nobody would pay her to do that—it's so easy.

There wouldn't be much good in teaching her to drive a cab, for where would she get a cab to drive? There aren't fathers and Diamonds everywhere."

"Perhaps if she were taught to be nice and clean, and only speak gentle words—"

"Mother could teach her that," interrupted Diamond.

"And to dress babies, and feed them, and take care of them," Mr. Raymond proceeded, "she might get a place as a nurse somewhere, you know. People do give money for that."

"Then I'll ask Mother," said Diamond.

"But you'll have to feed her too; and your father, not being strong, already has enough to manage without that."

"But I can help," said Diamond. "When he's tired of driving, up I get. And it doesn't make any difference to old Diamond. He goes about his work whether it's me or father driving him."

"Your father must be a good man, Diamond."

"Of course," said Diamond. "How could he drive a cab if he wasn't?"

"There are some men who drive cabs who are not very good," objected Mr. Raymond.

Diamond remembered the drunken cabman and saw that his friend was right.

"Ah, but," he returned, "he *must* be, you know, with such a horse as old Diamond."

"That does make a difference," agreed Mr. Raymond. "But it is quite enough that he is a good man without our having to explain it. Now, I think him a good man too, and here is how I am going to show it. I have to go on a trip for three months. I am going to rent my house to a man who does not want the use of my coach. My horse, I think, is nearly as old as your Diamond and I don't want him to be idle while I am gone, but neither do I want him worked too hard. So I have been thinking that perhaps your father would take charge of him while I am gone. Will you ask him to call and have a little chat with me when he comes home today?"

"Very well, sir. I will tell him. You can be sure he will come. My father thinks you a very kind gentleman, and I know he is right."

Mr. Raymond smiled, and as they had now reached his door, they parted, and Diamond went home. When his father entered the house, Diamond immediately gave him Mr. Raymond's message. His father said little, and as soon as he had finished his meal, rose, and went to see Diamond's friend.

He was shown at once into Mr. Raymond's study, where he gazed with some wonder at the many books on the walls and thought what an educated man Mr. Raymond must be.

Presently Mr. Raymond entered. He said much the same thing as he had told Diamond about his old horse, and then made the following proposal—that Joseph should have the use of Mr. Raymond's horse while he was away, on the condition that he never worked him more than six hours a day, and fed him well, and that, besides, he should take Nanny home as soon as she was able to leave the hospital, and provide for her as one of his own children—so long as he had the horse.

Diamond's father could not help thinking it was not overly advantageous to him, for he would have both the girl and the horse to feed, and only six hours work out of the horse in order to pay for the extra food. So he went home and recounted the proposal to his wife, saying that he didn't think there would be much to be gained from it.

"Not much in the way of money," said Diamond's mother, "but there is another advantage. Just think of what it would mean to the poor girl who hasn't a home to go to."

"She *is* one of Diamond's friends," mused his father.

"I could teach her housework," the mother went on, "and how to handle a baby. And besides, it would help me."

"I'm ashamed I did not think of both sides at once," said her husband. "Have the girl, by all means. I wonder if the horse is a great eater. To be sure, if I gave old Diamond two extra hours rest, it would be all the better for his old bones. And it would give Diamond something to do. He could drive old Diamond after dinner, and I could take the other horse out for six hours after tea, or in the morning, as I found best. It might pay the keep of both of them after all—that is if I had good luck. And Mr. Raymond has been very kind to our Diamond, hasn't he? And I would like to repay him."

"He has indeed, Joseph," said his wife, and there the conversation ended.

Diamond's father went the very next day to Mr. Raymond and accepted his proposal. So by the following week he had two horses instead of one. Oddly enough, the name of the new horse was Ruby, for he was a very red chestnut. Diamond's name came from a white star on his forehead. Young Diamond said they really *were* rich now, with such a big diamond and such a big ruby.

# Chapter Twenty-One

# Nanny's Dream

Nanny was not fit to be moved for some time yet and Diamond went to see her as often as he could. One evening as he sat by her bedside she said to him:

"I've had such a beautiful dream, Diamond. I would like to tell you about it."

"Oh do!" said Diamond. "I so like dreams."

"I was dressed in rags as I used to be, and I had great holes in my shoes and the mud came through to my feet. I didn't mind it as much as I used to, though. And there was a great red sunset, with streaks of gold and green. I wondered why I couldn't live in the sunset instead of in that dirt. Why was it always so far away always? Why did the sunset never come into our dirty street? And then it faded away, as the sunsets always do, and then a cold wind began to blow and flutter my rags about—"

"That was North Wind herself," interrupted Diamond.

"Eh?" said Nanny, and went on with her story.

"I turned my back to it and wandered away. I did not know where I was going, only it was warmer to go that way. I don't think it was a north wind, for I found myself in the west end. But it doesn't matter in a dream which wind it was."

"I believe North Wind can get into our dreams and blow in

them," said Diamond. "Sometimes she has blown me out of a dream altogether. But go on with your story. I think I like dreams even better than fairy tales. But they must be nice ones, like yours, you know."

"Well, I kept walking, keeping my back to the wind, until I came to a nice street on the top of a hill. How it happened I don't know, but the front door of one of the houses was open, and the back door as well, so that I could see right through the house into a garden place with green grass, and the moon shining on it. Think of that! I kicked my dirty shoes off and ran on my bare feet, up the steps, through the house, and on to the grass. And the moment I came into the moonlight I began to feel better.

"That's why North Wind blew you there," said Diamond.

"It must have come of Mr. Raymond's story about Princess Daylight," returned Nanny. "Well, I lay down on the grass in the moonlight without thinking of how I would get out of the place again. Somehow the moon suited me exactly. There was not a breath of the north wind you talk about."

"You didn't need her anymore, right then. She never goes where she's not needed," said Diamond. "But she blew you into the moonlight anyhow."

"Well, we won't argue about it," said Nanny. "Besides, you've got a tile loose, you know."

"What do you mean?"

"You know, they call you God's baby. They say you aren't right in the head."

"Well, suppose I do have a tile loose," returned Diamond; "don't you see, it may let in the moonlight, or the sunlight, for that matter?"

"Perhaps yes, perhaps no," said Nanny.

"And you've got your dreams too, Nanny."

"Yes, but I know they're dreams."

"So do I. But I know they are something more as well."

"Well, I don't."

"Perhaps you will someday," said Diamond.

Then Nanny resumed her story.

"I lay a long time and the moonlight got in at every tear in my clothes and made me feel so happy—"

"There, I tell you!" interrupted Diamond.

"What do you tell me?" returned Nanny.

"North Wind—"

"It was the moonlight, I tell you," persisted Nanny, and Diamond said no more.

"All at once I felt that the moon was not shining so strong. I looked up and there were clouds blowing over it. Up came the clouds faster and faster until the moon was covered up. So it grew very dark and a dog began to bark in the house. Then the dog ran out into the garden and I was afraid. So I jumped up and ran for a little summer house in the corner of the garden. The dog came after me, but I shut the door and was safe inside. And what do you think?—All at once there was the moon beginning to shine again—but only through one of the panes—a red one just the color of the sunset which had begun the dream. The moon was so beautiful and it grew larger and larger till it filled all the windows, and the summer house was nearly as bright as day. The dog stopped barking, and I heard a gentle tapping at the door, like the wind blowing a little branch against it."

"Just like her," said Diamond, who thought everything strange and beautiful must be done by North Wind.

"So I turned from the window and opened the door; and what do you think I saw?"

"A beautiful lady," said Diamond.

"No—the moon itself, as big as a house and as round as a ball. It stood on the grass—down right on the grass. It was so bright I could see nothing else. And as I stared, a door opened in the side of it, near the ground, and a curious little old man, with a crooked thing over his shoulder, looked out and said: 'Come along, Nanny; my lady wants to see you. We've come to fetch you.' I wasn't a bit frightened. I went up to the beautiful bright thing, and the old man held down his hand, and I took hold of it and gave a jump, and he gave me a lift, and I was inside the moon.

"And what do you think it was like? It was such a pretty little house, with blue windows and white curtains. The little man closed the door behind me, and began to pull at a rope which hung behind it with a weight at the end. After he had pulled a while, he said, 'There, that will do.' Then he took me by the hand and opened a little trapdoor in the floor and led me down two or three steps, and I saw a huge hole below me. 'Don't be frightened,' said the little man; 'it's not a hole. It's only a window. Put your face down and look through.' I did as he told me, and there was the garden and the summer house, far away, lying at the bottom of the moonlight, 'There!' said the little man; 'we've brought you up. Do you see the little dog barking at us down in the garden?'

"Then he took me up and up again by a little stair in a corner of the room, and through another trapdoor, and there was one great round window above us, and I saw the blue sky and the clouds and such a lot of stars, all so big and shining as hard as they could. The little man took me all round the house, and made me look out of every window. Oh, it was beautiful! There we were, all up in the air, in such a nice, clean little house! 'Your work will be to keep the windows bright,' said the little man. 'You won't find it too difficult, for there isn't much dust up here. Only the frost settles on them sometimes and the drops of rain leave marks on them.' 'I can easily clean them inside,' I said, 'but how am I to get the frost and rain off the outside of them?' 'Oh!' he said, 'it's quite easy. There are ladders all about. You only have to go out at the door and climb about. There are a great many windows you haven't seen yet, and some of them look into places you don't know anything about. I used to clean them myself, but I am getting rather old, you see.'

"After this he said nothing for a while, and I laid myself on the floor of his attic, and stared up and around at the great blue beautifulness of the sky through the window above me. I had almost forgotten him when he said, 'Are you through yet?' 'Through what?' I asked. 'Through saying your prayers,' he said. 'I wasn't saying my prayers,' I answered. 'Oh yes, you were,' he said, 'though you didn't know it. And now I have to show you something else.'

"He took my hand and led me down the stair again, and through a narrow passage, and through another, and another, and another. I don't know how there could be room for so many passages in such a little house. The center of it must have been farther from the sides than they were from each other, because it was bigger inside than it looked from the outside. It was funny—wasn't it, Diamond?"

"No," said Diamond. He was going to say that was just the sort of thing that always happened at the back of the north wind.

" 'Now I've showed you all I can tonight,' said the man. I followed him and he made me sit down under a lamp that hung from the roof, and gave me some bread and honey. How long I sat after I was through eating I don't know. The little man was busy about the room, pulling a string here, and a string there, but mainly the string at the back of the door. I was thinking nervously that he would soon be wanting me to go out and clean the windows, and I wasn't looking forward to the job. At last he came up to me with a great armful of rags. 'It's time you were starting on the windows,' he said; 'for there's rain coming, and if they're clean before it starts, it can't spoil them.' I got up at once. 'Don't be afraid,' he said. 'You won't fall off. But you must be careful. Always hold on with one hand while you are rubbing with the other.' As he spoke he opened the door. I started back with a terrible fright, for there was nothing but blue air to be seen under me, like a great ocean with no bottom at all. But I had to do what I had to do, and to live up here was so much nicer than down in the mud with holes in my shoes, so that I never thought of not doing as I was told. The little man showed me how and where to lay hold while I put my foot round the edge of the door onto the first rung of a ladder. 'Once you're up,' he said, 'you'll see how to do it well enough.' I did as he told me and crept up the ladder very carefully. Then he handed me the bundle of rags.

"I did the best I could, and crawled to the top of the moon. But what a grand sight it was! The stars were all over my head, so bright and so near that I could almost have reached out and touched them. It was so beautiful that all fear left me and I set to work diligently. I cleaned window after window. After a long while, there was a window that was just out of my reach. I stretched out my arm toward it, but my foot slipped and I gave a little cry. I reached all the harder and just managed to grab the sill of the window and held on tight. Presently the little man appeared on the other side of the window. He opened it and reached out to take my hand. I felt him tugging at it to pull me up toward him. I tried to speak to him, but, after a terrible effort, could only manage a groan. Other things began to come into my head. Somebody else had a hold of me. The little man wasn't there. I opened my eyes at last and saw the nurse. I had cried out in my sleep and she had come and waked me and was now holding my hand."

"It was a beautiful dream! Wasn't it, Nanny? What a pity you slipped and had to wake up. You might have had such a long dream and had such nice talks with the moon man. And you never did meet the man's lady yet. Although I know who she is. Do try to go there again, Nanny. I want to hear more about it."

"You silly baby! It was only a dream. I shall never have the chance."

"I don't know that," said Diamond. "How can you tell that a dream won't come again?"

"It's not likely."

"I don't know that," said Diamond.

"You're always saying that," said Nanny.

But now the nurse came and told him it was time to go; and Diamond went, saying to himself, "I can't help thinking that North Wind had something to do with that dream. Perhaps if she hadn't woken up, the moon might have carried her to the back of the north wind—who knows?"

# Chapter Twenty-Two

# Diamond and Ruby

It was a great delight to Diamond when finally Nanny was well enough to leave the hospital and go home to their house. She was not very strong yet, but Diamond's mother was very considerate and took good care of her. As Nanny got better and the color came back into her cheeks, her step grew lighter and quicker and she smiled more often and it was clear she would be a great help. It was great fun to see Diamond teaching her how to hold the baby and wash him and dress him. But it did not take long before she was able to do nearly as well as Diamond himself.

Things, however, did not go well with Joseph from the very day of Ruby's arrival. It almost seemed the red horse had brought bad luck with him. After the first month he fell lame and was unable to work for another whole month. And it was hardly any better after Ruby was able to work again, for it was a time of great depression in the business of the city and that is very soon felt among the cabmen. The fares were fewer and the pay less. Besides, it was a very rainy autumn and bread rose in price. When I add to all this the news that Diamond's mother was not feeling well from expecting another new baby, you will see that these were very hard times for our friends in the mews. During those days they lived on very short supply indeed.

Thus the three months passed by, but Mr. Raymond did not return. Joseph had been looking anxiously for him in order to get rid of Ruby, even though Nanny was a great help in the house. It was, in fact, a comfort to him to think that when the new baby did come, Nanny would be with his wife.

Of all God's gifts a baby is one of the greatest. Therefore it is no wonder that when this one came she was welcomed as heartily as if she had brought plenty with her. Of course she made a great difference in the work to be done, but Nanny was no end of help, and Diamond was as much of a sunbeam as ever and began to sing to the new baby the first moment he got her in his arms. But he did not sing the same songs to her that he had sung to his brother, for, he said, she was a sister baby and not a brother baby, and of course would not like the same kinds of songs. What the difference in his songs was, however, I do not pretend to be able to say.

How they managed to get through the long, dreary, expensive winter, I can hardly say. Sometimes things were better, sometimes worse. But at last the spring came and the winter was over and gone. Still Mr. Raymond did not return.

One week at last was worse than they had yet had. They almost had nothing to eat by the time it was over, and no money to buy more bread. But the sadder he saw his father and mother, the more Diamond set himself to sing to the two babies.

One thing that had increased their expenses was that they had to rent another little room for Nanny. When the second baby came, Diamond gave up his room so that Nanny might be near to help his mother. He then went to hers, which, although a finer place than Nanny had been accustomed to, was not particularly nice in Diamond's eyes. But he did not mind the change, for was it not a help to his mother? And was not Nanny more comfortable too? Therefore, the change was a happy one for everyone.

It was Friday night, and Diamond, like the rest of the household, had very little to eat that day. His mother would always pay the week's rent before she spent anything on food. His father had been very gloomy—so gloomy that he had actually been cross to his wife. It is a strange thing how the pain of seeing the suffering of those we love will sometimes make us add to their suffering by being cross with them. Consequently, Diamond had gone to bed very quiet and thoughtful and even a little troubled.

It had been a very stormy winter. And even now that spring had come, the north wind often blew. When Diamond went to his bed, which was in a tiny room in the roof, he heard it like the sea moaning, and when he fell asleep he still heard the moaning. All at once he said to himself, "Am I awake, or am I asleep?" But he had no time to answer the question, for there was North Wind calling him. His heart beat very fast, it was such a long time since he had heard that voice. He jumped out of bed and looked everywhere, but could not see her.

"Diamond, come here," she said again and again. But where the *here* was he could not tell.

"Dear North Wind," said Diamond, "I want so much to go to you, but I can't tell where you are."

"Come here, Diamond," was her only answer.

Diamond opened the door and went out of the room and down the stair and into the yard. His little heart was in a flutter, for he had long ago given up all thought of seeing her again. But when he got outside, a great puff of wind came against him, and in obedience to it he turned his back and went in the direction it was blowing. It blew him right up to the stable door, and kept on blowing.

"She wants me to go into the stable," said Diamond to himself, "but the door is locked."

He knew where the key was, in a certain hole in the wall—way too high for him to get at. He ran to the place, however, and just as he reached it there came a wild blast of wind, and down fell the key clanging on the stones at his feet. He picked it up and ran back to the stable door and went in.

A little light came through the dusty window from a gas lamp, enough to show him Diamond and Ruby with their two heads up, looking at each other across the partition of their stalls. The light showed the white mark on Diamond's forehead.

But what do you think he heard?

He heard the two horses talking to each other in a strange

language, which yet somehow or other he could understand. The first words he heard were from Diamond, who apparently had already been quarreling with Ruby.

"You ought to be ashamed of yourself, Ruby!" said old Diamond. "You are so plump and your skin shines so."

"There's no harm in being fat," said Ruby. "And I may as well shine as not."

"No harm?" retorted Diamond. "Is it no harm to go on eating up all poor master's oats when you only work six hours, and, as I hear, go no faster than a big dray horse with two cons behind him?—so they tell me."

"Your master's not mine," said Ruby. "I must attend to my own master's interests, and eat all that is given me, be as sleek and fat as I can, and go no faster than I need to."

"If the rest of the horses weren't all asleep, I do believe they would kick you out of the stable. You make me ashamed to be a horse. You dare to say my master isn't your master! That's your gratitude for the way he feeds and takes care of you!"

"He doesn't do it for my sake. If I were his own horse, he would work me as hard as he does you."

"And I'm proud to be worked hard. I wouldn't be as fat as you, not for all you're worth. You're a disgrace to the stable. Look at the horse next to you. *He's* something like a horse—all skin and bone. And his master isn't over kind to him either. He put a stinging lash on his whip last week. But that old horse knows his driver's got the wife and children to keep, as well as his drunken master, and he works like a horse."

"Well, at least you ought to be thankful you get two hours of rest a day because I'm here," said Ruby.

"I thank my master for that—not you, you lazy fellow! I don't even believe you were lame at all."

"Oh, but I was."

"Then it was your own fault. I was never lame in all my life. You don't take care of your legs. You never lay them down at night. There you are with your huge frame crushing down your poor legs all night long. You are a horse indeed!"

"But I tell you I *was* lame. I put my foot on one of those horrid stones they make the roads with, and it gave my ankle such a twist."

"So long as you don't lift your feet better, but fall asleep between every step, you'll run a good chance of laming all your ankles. It's not a lively horse that comes to grief in that way. I tell you, I believe it wasn't much, and if it was, it was your own fault. Now, I'm going to sleep. I'll try to think as well of you as I can. If you would but step out a bit and run off a little of your fat!"

Here Diamond began to double up his knees to lie down. But Ruby spoke again, in what young Diamond thought to be a rather different tone.

"I say, Diamond, I can't bear to have an honest old horse like you think of me like that. I will tell you the truth: it was my own fault that I fell lame. I meant to do it, Diamond."

"You unworthy wretch! You, a horse! Why did you do that?"

"Because I wanted to grow fat."

"You grease tub! I thought you were a humbug! Why did you want to get fat? But there's no truth to be got out of you. You aren't fit to be a horse!"

"Because I didn't know when master might come home and want to see me."

"You good-for-nothing brute! You wanted to look handsome, did you? Keep out of my way or I'll bite you!"

"But you're a good horse, Diamond. You can't hurt me."

"Can't hurt you! Just let me once try."

"No, you can't."

"Why, then?"

"Because I'm an angel."

"What?"

"Of course you don't know."

"Indeed I don't."

"I know you don't. You're just an old human horse, and you couldn't know. But there's young Diamond listening to all we're saying, and he knows well enough that there are horses in heaven for angels to ride upon, as well as other animals. And the horses the angels ride must be angel horses, otherwise the angels couldn't ride upon them. Well, I'm one of them."

"You aren't."

"Did you ever know a horse to tell a lie?"

"Never before. But you've already confessed to pretending to be lame."

"Nothing of the sort. It was necessary I should grow fat, and necessary that good Joseph, your master, should grow lean. I could have pretended to be lame, but that no horse, least of all an angel horse, would do. So I *had* to be lame, and so I sprained my ankle. And it hurt me very much, I assure you, though you may not be good enough to believe it."

Old Diamond made no reply. He had lain down and a sleepy snort, very much like a snore, revealed that, if he was not already asleep, he was almost so. When young Diamond heard this, he thought he might venture to pick up the conversation.

"I'm good enough to believe it, Ruby," he said.

But Ruby never turned his head or took any notice of him. I suppose he did not understand English, even though Diamond had been able to understand their horse language. But finding that his companion made no reply, Ruby stuck his head over the partition and looking down at old Diamond said:

"You just wait until tomorrow, and you'll see whether or not I'm an angel horse.—I declare the old horse is fast asleep!—Diamond!"

Ruby turned away and began pulling the hay from his hay-rack in silence. Young Diamond gave a shiver, and looking around saw that the door of the stable was open. He began to feel as if he had been dreaming, and after a glance about the stable to see if North Wind was anywhere to be seen, he thought he had better go back to bed.

## Chapter Twenty-Three

# The Prospect Brightens

The next morning, Diamond's mother said to her husband, "I'm not comfortable about Diamond again. I'm afraid he's getting back into his odd ways. He's been at his old trick of walking in his sleep. I saw him run up the stairs in the middle of the night."

"Didn't you follow him?"

"Of course I did—and found him fast asleep in his bed. It's because he's had so little to eat, I'm afraid."

"That may be. And I'm sorry. But if it doesn't please God to send us enough, what am I to do?"

"You can't help it, I know, my dear good man," returned Martha. "And I don't know why he shouldn't get on as well as the rest of us. Here I am nursing the baby all this time, and I'm feeling pretty well. But to hear the little man singing, you wouldn't think there was anything wrong with him."

For at that moment Diamond was singing like a lark in the clouds. He had the new baby in his arms.

"Think of a fat angel, Dulcimer!" said Diamond.

The baby had not been named yet, but Diamond, in reading

his Bible, had come upon the word *dulcimer* and thought it so pretty that always after that he called his sister Dulcimer.

"Think of a red fat angel, Dulcimer!" he repeated, "for Ruby's an angel of a horse. He sprained his ankle and got fat on purpose."

"What purpose, Diamond?" asked his father.

"Ah, that I don't know. I suppose to look handsome when his master comes," answered Diamond.—"What do you think, Dulcimer? It must be for some good, for Ruby's an angel."

"I wish I were rid of him anyhow," said his father. "It was unfortunate for his owner to leave him on my hands this way."

"Perhaps he couldn't help it," suggested Diamond. "I'm sure he had a good reason for it."

"And we don't know what may come of it yet, Husband," said his wife. "Mr. Raymond may give you a little extra, seeing you've had him for longer than you bargained for."

Joseph rose and went to get his cab out, and Diamond resumed his singing. Where he got the words I cannot tell.

"You didn't make that song, did you, Diamond?" asked his mother when he was finished.

"No, Mother. I wish I had. No, I didn't. That would be to take it from somebody else. But it's mine anyway."

"What makes it yours?"

"Because I love it so much."

"Does loving a thing make it yours?"

"I think so, Mother—at least more than anything else can. If I didn't love baby she wouldn't be mine a bit. But I do love baby, and baby is my very own Dulcimer."

"The baby's mine, Diamond."

"That makes her all the more mine, Mother, because I love you too, and so you are mine. Love makes the only *myness*," said Diamond.

When his father came home to have his dinner, and to change Diamond for Ruby, he looked very sad and he told them he had not had a fare worth mentioning the whole morning.

"We shall all have to go to the poorhouse, Wife," he said.

"It would be better to go to the back of the north wind," said Diamond dreamily, not intending to say it aloud.

"So it would," answered his father. "But how are we to get there, Diamond?"

"We must wait till we're taken," returned Diamond.

Before his father could speak again, a knock came to the door, and in walked Mr. Raymond with a smile on his face. Joseph got up and received him respectfully. Martha set a chair for him, but he would not sit down.

"You seem rather glum," he said to Joseph. "You are not glad to see me, for you don't want to part with the old horse?"

"Indeed, sir, just the opposite. I've wished I were rid of him a thousand times these last eight or nine months."

"I'm sorry to hear that," said Mr. Raymond. "Hasn't he been of service to you?"

"Not much, not with his lameness."

"Ah, he's been lame, has he?" said Mr. Raymond.

"It wasn't my fault, and he's all right now. I wasn't working him hard. I don't know how it happened."

"He did it on purpose," said Diamond. "He put his foot on a stone just to twist his ankle."

"How do you know that, Diamond?" said his father, turning to him. "I never told you that."

"I heard it—in the stable," answered Diamond.

"Let's have a look at him," said Mr. Raymond.

"If you'll step into the yard," said Joseph, "I'll bring him out."

They went and Joseph walked Ruby into the middle of the yard.

"Why," said Mr. Raymond, "he's grown fat as a pig!"

"I couldn't work him for a whole month, and he did nothing but eat his head off. He's an awful eater. I've worked him the best part of six hours a day since, but I could hardly make the most of that for fear of his getting hurt again. And he goes so slow all the time, I'm glad you've come for him."

"Suppose I were to ask you to buy him from me—cheap."

"I wouldn't take him if you gave him to me, sir. He's nearly brought me to beggary with his snail's pace."

"Then bring out your own horse, and let me see what sort of a pair they'd make."

Joseph laughed and went to fetch Diamond.

When the two were placed side-by-side, beside the great red round barrel Ruby, Diamond looked like nothing but bones with skin thrown over it. Gaunt and grim and tired he stood, kissing his master, and paying attention to no one else.

"He's so thin," said Mr. Raymond. "You've been working him *too* hard."

"This horse is worth three of the other," returned Joseph.

"Well, I think they might make a very nice pair, although the one's too fat and the other too lean. So if you won't buy my Ruby, then I must buy your Diamond."

"I wouldn't part with my old Diamond no matter how full of bones his skin is."

"Who said anything about parting with him?"

"You did, sir."

"No, I didn't. I only spoke of buying him to make a pair with Ruby. We could thin down Ruby and fatten up Diamond a bit. They are nearly the same height. Of course, you would be my coachman, if you could only find a little love for Ruby in your heart."

Joseph stood bewildered, unable to answer.

"I've bought a small place in the country," continued Mr. Raymond, "and I need a pair of horses for my carriage. I think these two will do just fine, that is, if you could see your way clear to move your family from the city to work for me. Suppose for a week or two you try to thin down Ruby and bring Diamond up."

A strong desire to laugh, mingled with an inclination to cry, rose within Joseph, which made it all the harder for him to speak.

"I beg your pardon, sir," he said finally. "I've been so miserable that many's the time I've grumbled about you and your Ruby. But whenever I said anything my little Diamond would look at me with a smile, as much as to say: 'I know him better than you, Father,' and upon my word, I always thought the boy must be right."

"Will you sell me old Diamond, then?"

"I will, sir, on one condition—that if you ever want to part with him or me, you will give me the option of buying him back. I could *not* part with him, sir. As to who's his owner, that doesn't matter. For, as Diamond says, it's only loving a thing that can make it yours—and I do love old Diamond, sir, dearly."

"Well, here's a check for twenty pounds for him. Will that be enough?"

"It's too much, sir. His heart is worth millions—but this is too much to pay for his body, sir."

"I don't think so. Especially after you feed him up again. You take it, and continue on with your cabbing for another month. Only let Diamond rest and work Ruby the hardest. By that time I will be ready for you to go down into the country with me."

"Thank you, sir, thank you. Diamond knew you were a friend the moment he saw you. I do believe that child of mine knows more than most people."

"I think so too," said Mr. Raymond as he walked away.

He had had no intention of being gone so long. But he had become sick in Switzerland and had not been able to return sooner. He went away now very pleased at how Joseph had stood the test that had been put to him, and was a true man.

Joseph rushed in to his wife. When she heard that the two horses were to go together in double harness, she burst out laughing. "Why the notion of that great fat Ruby going side by side with our poor old Diamond!" she said.

"Why not, Mother?" said Diamond. "With a month's oats and little to do Diamond will begin to look Ruby's size. I think it's good for different sorts to go together. Now Ruby will have a chance to teach Diamond better manners."

"Are you saying our Diamond's not a gentleman?" said his father almost gruffly.

"I don't mean he isn't, Father. For I imagine some gentlemen judge their neighbors unjustly. That's all I mean. Diamond shouldn't have thought such bad things of Ruby. He didn't try to make the best of him."

"How do you know that?"

"I heard them talking one night."

"Who?"

"Diamond and Ruby. Ruby's an angel."

Joseph stared at his son and said no more. For all his joy at the prospect of a new and steady job, he was gloomy as he harnessed the angel for the day's work, for he thought his darling Diamond was going out of his mind.

He could not help thinking rather differently, however, when he found the change that had come over Ruby. Considering how fat he was, he exerted himself wonderfully and made much better speed than before. Within no time at all Joseph's earlier dislike of the horse had vanished, and he felt as if Ruby had been his friend all the time.

# Chapter Twenty-Four

# In the Country

Before the end of the month Ruby had gotten respectably thin and Diamond respectably stout. Joseph and his wife had gotten their affairs in order and everything was ready for moving at the shortest notice from Mr. Raymond. As for Nanny, she had been very happy since leaving the hospital, but she saw nothing so attractive about the idea of moving to the country with Diamond's family. She hardly even knew what the word *country* meant, for all her life she had seen nothing but streets. Besides, she was still more attracted to her friend Jim than to Diamond: Jim was a reasonable being, but Diamond in her eyes was hardly more than an overgrown baby who always said the strangest things.

"There ain't nothing in the country but the sun and moon, Diamond," she said one day while they were talking about the move.

"There's trees and flowers," said Diamond,

"Well, they don't count for much. I'd still rather stay in the city."

"But they're beautiful and make you happy to look at them."

"That's because you're such a silly."

Diamond smiled with a faraway look, as if he were gazing

through clouds of green leaves. But he was actually thinking of what more he could do for Nanny. That same evening he went to find Mr. Raymond, for he had heard he had returned to town.

"How are you, Diamond?" asked Mr. Raymond. "I am glad to see you."

And he was glad to see him indeed, for he had grown to like Diamond very much.

"What do you want now, my child?" he asked.

"There's a friend of Nanny's, a lame boy, called Jim."

"I've heard of him," said Mr. Raymond. "What about him?"

"Nanny doesn't want to go to the country, sir."

"And what has that to do with Jim?"

"You couldn't find some place for him to work in, could you, sir?"

"I don't know. Maybe I could. That is, if you can find good reason for it."

"He's a good boy, sir. A tall policeman helped me find him to tell him about where Nanny had gone. He can shine boots."

"I'm glad for that."

"You will want your boots shined in the country—won't you, sir?"

"Yes, to be sure."

"And with Jim there, Nanny would be more pleased to go. She's so fond of Jim. And besides cleaning boots, he could do odd jobs for you too, sir."

"Well, you come right to the point, Diamond. I will think about it. In the meantime, can you bring Jim to see me?"

"I'll try, sir. But they don't pay much attention to me. They think I'm silly in the head," added Diamond with one of his sweetest smiles.

What Mr. Raymond thought I dare hardly attempt to put down here. But one thing he thought was that the wisest people must often appear foolish to those who don't share their wisdom.

Diamond succeeded in bringing Jim to visit Mr. Raymond, and in the end he decided to give the boy a chance. He provided new clothes for both him and Nanny, and not many days later Joseph took his wife and three children and Nanny and Jim by train to a certain station in the county of Yent, where they found a cart waiting to take them and their luggage to The Mound, which was the name of Mr. Raymond's new house. That same night Joseph returned to town and the following morning drove Ruby and Diamond down, with the carriage behind them, and Mr. Raymond and a lady in the carriage. Mr. Raymond had married and was bringing his new wife to live at The Mound.

The weather was very hot, and the woods very shadowy. There were not a great many wild flowers, for it was getting well toward autumn. But there was plenty of the loveliest grass and daisies about the house, and one of Diamond's greatest pleasures was to lie on the grass with the daisies all about and breathe the pure air. But all the time he was dreaming of the country at the back of the north wind and trying to remember the songs the river used to sing. For this place was more like being at the back of the north wind than anything he had known since he had left it.

Diamond did not do so much for his mother now, because Nanny did most of his former jobs. But he still helped his father, both in the stable and in the harness room. And usually he went with him up on the box of the carriage that he might learn to drive two horses and be ready to open the carriage door. Mr. Raymond advised the boy's father to give his son plenty of liberty.

"A special boy like that," he said, "ought not to be pushed."

Joseph agreed heartily, smiling to himself at the idea of pushing Diamond. After doing everything that fell to him, the boy had huge amounts of free time at his disposal. And a merry time it was for him. Only for two months, he neither saw nor heard anything of North Wind.

Mr. Raymond's house was called The Mound because it stood upon a steep little knoll. It had originally been built as a hunting lodge, because from it you could see all the country for miles around. Joseph and his wife lived in a little cottage a short way from the house. It was a real cottage, with a roof of thick thatch. At first Diamond had a little nest of a room under this thatch, but after a while Mr. and Mrs. Raymond wanted to have him for a page, or helper, in the house, and his father and mother were pleased to have him do it. So he was dressed in a suit of blue and moved to a new room in the house.

"Would you be afraid to sleep alone, Diamond?" asked his mistress.

"I never was afraid of anything that I can remember—not much at least," said Diamond.

"There's a little room at the top of the house—all alone," she said. "Perhaps you would not mind sleeping there?"

"I like it best up high. Will I be able to see out?"

"I will show you the place," she answered, and taking him by the hand she led him up and up the winding stairway in one of the two towers of the house. Near the top they entered a tiny little room, with two windows from which you could see over the whole countryside. Diamond clapped his hands with delight.

"You like this room, then, Diamond?" asked his mistress.

"It's the grandest room in the whole house," he answered. "I shall be near the stars, and yet not far from the tops of the trees." He also thought it would be a nice place for North Wind to come to visit him, but he said nothing about that.

It was very soon after this that I came to know Diamond. I was then a tutor, or teacher, in a family whose property was next to the Raymonds'. I had met Mr. Raymond in London some time before and was walking up the drive toward his house to call upon him one fine warm evening when I saw Diamond for the first time. He was sitting at the foot of a great beech tree a few yards from the road with a book on his knees. He did not see me at first. I walked up behind the tree, and looking over his shoulder I saw that he was reading a fairy-tale book.

"What are you reading?" I asked. Diamond turned his head as quietly as if he were only obeying his mother's voice, not appearing startled in the least.

"I am reading the story of the Little Lady and the Goblin Prince," said Diamond.

"I am sorry I don't know the story," I returned. "Who is it by?"

"Mr. Raymond made it."

"Is he your uncle?" I asked, guessing.

"No, he's my master."

"What do you do for him?" I asked.

"Anything he wishes me to do," he answered. "I am busy for him now. He gave me this story to read. He wants my opinion on it."

"Don't you find it rather hard to make up your mind?"

"Oh dear no! Any story always tells me itself what I'm to think about it. Mr. Raymond doesn't want me to say whether it is a clever story or not, but whether I like it, and why I like it. I never can tell what they call clever from what they call silly, but I always know whether I like a story or not."

"And can you always tell why you like it or not?"

"No. Very often I can't tell at all. Sometimes I can. I always know, but I can't always tell why. Mr. Raymond writes the stories, and then tries them on me. Mother does the same when she makes jam. She's made such a lot of jam since we came here. And she always makes me taste it to see if it'll do. Mother knows by the face I make whether it will or not."

At this moment I caught sight of two more children approaching. One was a handsome girl, the other a pale-faced, awkward-looking boy, who limped on one leg. I backed up a little to see what they would do, for they seemed a little upset about something. After a few hurried words with my new friend they all went off together, and I continued on my way to the house, where I was kindly received by Mr. and Mrs. Raymond. From them I learned more of Diamond, and was therefore all the more glad to find him seated in the same place when I returned.

"What did the boy and girl want with you, Diamond?" I asked.

"They had seen a creature that frightened them."

"And they came to tell you about it?"

"They couldn't get water out of the well because of it. So they wanted me to go with them."

"They're both older than you."

"Yes, but they were frightened of it."

"And you weren't frightened of it?"

"No."

"Why?"

"Because I'm silly, I'm never frightened at things."

"And what was it?" I asked.

"I think it was a kind of angel—a very little one. It had a long body and great wings. It flew backward and forward over the well, or hung right in the middle, as if its business was to take care of the water."

"And what did you do to scare it away?"

"I didn't scare it away. I knew whatever the creature was, the well was to get water out of. So I took the jug, dipped it in, and drew out the water."

"And what did the creature do?"

"Flew about."

"And it didn't hurt you?"

"No. Why should it? I wasn't doing anything wrong."

"What did your friends say then?"

"They said, 'Thank you, Diamond. What a dear silly you are!' "

"And you weren't angry with them?"

"No. Why should I be? I would like it if they played with me a little. But they never heed me. I don't mind it much though. The other creatures are friendly. They don't run away from me. Only they're so busy with their own work, they don't mind me much."

"Do you feel lonely then?"

"Oh no! When nobody minds me, I get into my nest and look up. And then the sky does mind me, and thinks about me."

"Where is your nest?"

He rose, saying, "I will show you," and led me to the other

side of the tree. There hung a little rope ladder from one of the lower branches. The boy climbed up the ladder and got upon the branch. Then he climbed farther into the leafy branches and went out of sight.

After a little while I heard his voice coming down out of the tree. "I am in my nest now," said the voice.

"I can't see you," I returned.

"I can't see you either, but I can see the first star peeping out of the sky. I would like to get up into the sky. Don't you think I shall someday?"

"Yes, I do. Tell me more what you see up there."

"I don't see anything more, except a few leaves and the big sky over me. It goes swinging about. The earth is all behind my back. There comes another star! The wind is like kisses from a big lady. When I get up here I feel as if I were in North Wind's arms."

This was the first I heard of North Wind.

The whole way and look of the child, so full of quiet wisdom and yet so ready to accept the judgment of others about his oddity, took hold of my heart, and I felt myself wonderfully drawn toward him. It seemed to me somehow as if little Diamond possessed the secret of life and was himself an angel of God with something special to say or do. A gush of reverence came over me, and with a single *good night,* I turned and left him in his nest.

I saw him often after this and we became such good friends that eventually he told me all that I have told you. I cannot pretend to explain everything. The easiest way to explain him was that of Nanny and Jim, who said to each other that Diamond had a tile loose in his head, which meant they thought him just a little crazy. But Mr. Raymond shared my opinion concerning the boy, that there was something very special about him. And Mrs. Raymond said that she often rang the bell to send for him just to have the pleasure of seeing the lovely stillness of the boy's face, with those blue eyes which seemed to have been made for other people to look into instead of for him to look out of.

One very strange thing is that I could never find out where he got the many songs he sang. At times they would be but bubbles blown out of a nursery rhyme, as was the following, which I heard him sing one evening to his little Dulcimer.

Little Bo Peep, she lost her sheep,
And didn't know where to find them;
They were over the height and out of sight,
Trailing their tails behind them.

Little Bo Peep woke out of her sleep,
Jumped up and set out to find them:
"The silly things, they've got no wings,
And they've left their trails behind them.

"They've taken their tails, but they've left their trails,
And so I shall follow and find them."
For wherever a tail had dragged a trail,
The long grass grew behind them.

After the sun, like clouds they did run,
But she knew they were her sheep:
She sat down to cry, and look up at the sky,
But she cried herself fast asleep.

Never weep, Bo Peep, though you lose your sheep,
And do not know where to find them;
'Tis after the sun the mothers have run,
And there are their lambs coming back behind them.

Some of them were out of books Mr. Raymond had given him. These he always knew, but about the others he could seldom tell. Sometimes he would say, "I made that one up," but generally he would say, "I don't know; I found it somewhere," or, "I got it at the back of the north wind."

One evening I found him sitting on the grassy slope under the house with his Dulcimer in his arms and his little brother rolling on the grass beside them. He was chanting in his usual way, more like the sound of a brook than anything else I can think of. When I went up to them he ceased his chant.

"Do go on, Diamond. Don't mind me," I said.

He began again at once. While he sang, Nanny and Jim sat a little way off, but they paid little attention to Diamond. As Diamond went on singing, it grew very dark and just as he stopped there came a great flash of lightning that blinded us all for a moment. Dulcimer crowed with pleasure, but when the roar of thunder came after it, the little brother gave a loud cry of terror. Nanny and Jim came running up to us, pale with fear. Diamond's face, too, was paler than usual, but with delight. Some of the glory of the lightning seemed to have clung to it, and remained shining.

"You're not frightened—are you, Diamond?" I said.

"No. Why should I be?" he answered with his usual question, looking up in my face with calm shining eyes.

"He ain't got sense to be frightened," said Nanny, going up and giving him a pitying hug.

"Perhaps there's more sense in not being frightened, Nanny," I returned. "Do you think the lightning can do as it likes?"

"It might kill you," said Jim.

"Oh no, it won't!" said Diamond. As he spoke there came another great flash and a tearing crack.

"There's a tree struck!" I said, and when we looked around, after the blinding of the flash had left our eyes, we saw a huge branch of the beech tree, in which was Diamond's nest, hanging to the ground like the broken wing of a bird.

"There!" cried Nanny. "I told you so. If you had been up there you see what would have happened, you little silly!"

"No, I don't," replied Diamond, and began to sing to Dulcimer. Then there came a blast of wind, and the rain followed in straight, pouring lines. Diamond jumped up with his little Dulcimer in his arms, and Nanny caught up the little boy, and they ran for the cottage. Jim vanished with a double shuffle, and I went into the house.

When I came out again later in the evening to return home, the clouds were gone and the evening sky glimmered through the trees. I turned a little out of my way to look at the stricken tree. I saw the bough torn from the trunk, and that was all the dusky light would allow me to see. While I stood gazing, down from the sky came a sound of singing, but the voice was neither of lark nor of nightingale: it was sweeter than either—it was the voice of Diamond, up in what remained of his airy nest:

The lightning and thunder,
 They go and they come;
But the stars and the stillness
 Are always at home.

And then the voice ceased.

"Good night, Diamond," I said.

"Good night, sir," answered Diamond.

As I walked away thinking, I saw the great black top of the tree swaying about against the sky in the wind, and heard the murmur as of many dim half-clear voices filling the solitude around Diamond's nest.

## Chapter Twenty-Five

# Diamond Questions North Wind

You will not be surprised that after this I did my best to know Diamond better. And it was not difficult to gain his friendship, for he was so ready to trust everyone. But it took some time before he told me all about his relations with North Wind. I imagine he could not quite make up his mind what to think of them.

On an evening soon after the thunderstorm, in a late twilight, with a half moon high in the sky, I came upon Diamond climbing up his little ladder into the beech tree.

"Why are you always going up there, Diamond?" I heard Nanny ask rather rudely.

"Sometimes for one thing, sometimes for another, Nanny," answered Diamond, looking up into the sky as he climbed. "I'm going to look at the moon tonight."

"You'll see the moon just as well down here."

"I don't think so."

"You'll be no nearer to her up there."

"Oh yes, I will! I wish I could dream as pretty dreams about her as you can, Nanny."

"You silly! Will you never stop talking about that dream? I only dreamed one, and it was nonsense enough, I'm sure!"

"It wasn't nonsense. It was a beautiful dream—and a funny one too, both in one."

"But what's the good of talking about it that way when you know it was only a dream? Dreams aren't true."

"That one was true, Nanny. You know it was."

"I can't get any sense into him!" exclaimed Nanny, with an expression of despair. "Do you really believe, Diamond, that there's a house in the moon, with a crooked little man and windows in it?"

"If there isn't, there's something better," he answered, and vanished in the leaves over our heads.

I went into the house, where I visited often in the evenings. When I came out there was a little wind blowing, very pleasant after the heat of the day, for although it was late summer now, it was still hot. The treetops were swinging about in it. I walked past the beech tree and called up to see if Diamond was still in his nest in its rocking head.

"Are you there, Diamond?" I asked.

"Yes, sir," came his voice in reply.

"Isn't it getting too dark for you to get down safely?"

"Oh no, sir—if I take my time. I know my way so well, and I never let go with one hand till I've got a good hold with the other."

"Do be careful," I said—foolishly, seeing the boy was already being as careful as he could be.

"I'm coming," he returned. "I've got all the moon I want tonight."

I heard a rustling drawing nearer and nearer, and in a few minutes he appeared creeping down his little ladder. I took him in my arms and set him on the ground.

"Thank you, sir," he said. "That's the north wind blowing, isn't it, sir?"

"I can't tell," I answered. "It feels cool and kind, and I think it may be."

"I shall know when I get up to my own room," said Diamond, "I think I hear my mistress's bell. Good night, sir."

He ran to the house, and I went home.

His mistress had rung for him only because it was time for him to go to bed. She was very careful over him and I thought he was not looking very well. When he reached his own room he opened both his windows, one of which looked to the north and the other to the east, to find out which way the wind was blowing. It blew right in at the northern window. Diamond was very glad, for he thought perhaps North Wind herself might come now: a real strong north wind had not blown all the time since he had left London. But since she always came of herself and never when he was looking for her, he shut the east window and went to bed and fell fast asleep.

He woke in the middle of the night. The moon had disappeared and he thought he heard a knocking at his door. He jumped out of bed and ran to open it. But there was no one there.

He closed it again, but the noise was still there. He looked around and found that another door was rattling. It was the door to a closet that he had never been able to open. *Now,* he thought, *the wind blowing in at the window must be shaking it.*

He went to the closet door and found that now it opened quite easily. But to his surprise, when he looked in he did not see a closet at all but a long, narrow room. The moon was shining in at an open window at the farther end. He was so delighted at the discovery of this strange moonlit place so close to his own snug little room that he went in and began to dance about the floor. The wind came in through the door he had left open and blew about him as he danced, and he kept turning toward it so that it could blow in his face as he danced. He kept picturing to himself all the many places it had blown over on its way to The Mound—the hillsides and farmyards and treetops and meadows.

As he danced he grew more and more delighted with the motion and the wind. His feet grew stronger and his body lighter, and at length it seemed as if he were floating up on the air and could almost fly. Something made him look up, and to his unspeakable delight he found his uplifted hands lying in those of North Wind, who was dancing with him all around the long bare room. Her hair was one moment falling to the floor, the next filling the ceiling. Her eyes shone on him like thinking stars, and the sweetest of beautiful smiles played breezily about her mouth. She was the height of a rather tall lady but did not stoop to dance with him; she only held his hands high in hers. When he saw her he gave one jump, and his arms were about her neck and her arms holding him to her bosom. The very same moment she swept with him through the open window the moon was shining through, flew in a great circle through the sky, and landed with him in his nest on the top of the tree. There she placed him on her lap and began to speak to him as if he were her own baby, and Diamond was so entirely happy that he did not care to speak a word. At length, however, he found that he was going to sleep and he did not want to do that when he was with North Wind.

"Please, dear North Wind," he said, "I am so happy that I'm afraid it's a dream. How am I to know that it's not a dream?"

"What does it matter?" returned North Wind.

"I should cry," said Diamond.

"But why should you cry? If it is a dream, it is a nice one—isn't it?"

"That's just why I want it to be true."

"Have you forgotten what you said to Nanny about her dream?"

"It's not for the dream itself," answered Diamond, "for I can enjoy it whether it's a dream or not. It's for you, North Wind. I couldn't bear to find out that it's just a dream, for then I should lose you. You would be nobody then. You aren't a dream, are you, dear North Wind?"

"I'm either not a dream, or there's something better that's not a dream, Diamond," said North Wind, in a rather sorrowful tone, he thought.

"But it is not something better—it's you I want, North Wind," he persisted, beginning to cry a little.

She made no answer, but rose with him in her arms and sailed away over the treetops till they came to a meadow where a flock of sheep was feeding.

"Do you remember what the song you were singing a week

ago says about Bo Peep—how she lost her sheep when they ran after the sun, but found that she got even more lambs in return when they ran back to her?" asked North Wind, sitting down on the grass and placing him in her lap as before.

"Oh yes, I do," answered Diamond, "but I don't quite like that, for it makes it sound as if one thing's as good as another, or two new ones are better than one that's lost. But once you've looked into anybody's eyes, right deep down into them, I mean, nobody else will do for that one anymore. Nobody, no matter how beautiful or good, could ever take the place of that one. So you see, North Wind, I can't help being frightened to think that perhaps I am only dreaming and you are not real, after all. Do tell me that you are my own real beautiful North Wind."

Again she rose and shot herself up into the air and Diamond lay quietly in her arms, waiting for what she would say. He tried to see up into her face, for he was dreadfully afraid she was not answering him because she was a dream, after all. She had let her hair fall down over her face so that he could not see it, and this frightened him still more.

"Do speak, North Wind," he said at last.

"I never speak when I have nothing to say," she replied.

"Then I think you must be a real North Wind, and not a dream," said Diamond. "If you were to say one word to comfort me that wasn't true, then I would know you must be a dream, for a great beautiful lady like you could never tell a lie."

"But she might not know how to say what she had to say in a way that a little boy like you could understand it," said North Wind. "Here, let us get down again and I will try to tell you what I think. But I am not able to answer all your questions. There are a great many things I don't understand either."

She descended on a grassy little hill. There were some rabbits about in the moonlight, looking very sober and wise. When they saw North Wind, instead of turning around and running away with a thump of their heels, they cantered slowly up to her and snuffed all about her with their noses, which moved every way at once. That was their way of kissing her, and as she talked to Diamond, she would every now and then stroke down their furry backs or play with their long ears. Diamond thought they would have jumped up on her lap, except that he was already there.

"I think," she said after they had been sitting in silence for a while, "that if I was only a dream, you would not have been able to love me as you do. You love me even when you are not with me, don't you?"

"Indeed I do," answered Diamond, stroking her hand.

"You might have loved me in a dream, and then half forgotten me when you woke. But I don't think you could have loved me like a real person if I was just a dream. Even then, I don't think you could dream anything that hadn't something real like it somewhere. But you've seen me in many shapes, Diamond: you remember I was a wolf once—don't you?"

"Oh yes—a good wolf that frightened a naughty drunken nurse."

"Well, suppose I were to turn ugly, would you rather I wasn't a dream even then?"

"Yes. For I would know you were still beautiful inside all the same. You would love me and I would love you. I wouldn't like you to look ugly, you know. But I wouldn't believe it a bit."

"Not if you saw it, the ugliness I mean?"

"No, not if I saw it ever so plain."

"That's my Diamond! I will tell you all I know about it then. I don't think I am just what you think I am. I have to shape myself various ways to various people. But the heart of me is true. People sometimes call me by dreadful names, and they think they know all about me. But they don't. Sometimes they call me Bad Fortune, sometimes Evil Fate, sometimes Ruin, or Misery, or even D—." She stopped and Diamond thought her voice sounded sad. Then she continued. "They have another name for me which they think the most dreadful of all."

"What is that?" asked Diamond, smiling up in her face.

"I won't tell you that name. Do you remember having to go through me to get into the country at my back?"

"Oh yes, I do. How cold you were, North Wind! and so white, all but your lovely eyes! My heart grew like a lump of ice, and then I forgot for a while."

"You were very near knowing what they call me then. Would

you be afraid of me if you had to go through me again?"

"No. Why should I? Indeed, I would be glad to, if it was only to get another glimpse of the country at your back."

"You've never seen it yet."

"Haven't I? Oh, I thought I had. What did I see when I was there, then?"

"Only a picture of it. The real country at my real back is ever so much more beautiful than that. You shall see it one day—perhaps before very long."

"Do they sing songs there?"

"Where do you think all the songs come from in your dreams?"

"I thought you must have something to do with my dreams. Sometimes they are so beautiful. Did you give Nanny her dream too—about the moon and the crooked little man?"

"Yes."

"Oh, I'm glad. I was almost sure you had something to do with that too. And did you tell Mr. Raymond the story about Princess Daylight?"

"I believe I had something to do with it. In any event he thought about it one night when he couldn't sleep. But sometimes I'm unable to make you dream hard enough to remember the songs. I make you dream pictures, though. But you will hear the real songs themselves when you do get to the back of—"

"My own dear North Wind," said Diamond, finishing the sentence for her, and kissing the arm that held him leaning against her.

"And now we've settled all this—for the time being at least," said North Wind.

"You must wait and be hopeful, and be content with not being quite sure about my being a dream. Come now, I will take you home again, for it won't do to tire you too much."

"Oh no, no. I'm not tired in the least," pleaded Diamond.

"It is better, though."

"Very well, if you wish," yielded Diamond with a sigh.

"You are a dear good boy," said North Wind. "I will come for you again tomorrow night and take you out for a longer time. We shall make a little journey together. We shall start earlier, and as the moon will be later, we shall have moonlight all the way."

She rose and swept over the meadow and the trees. In a few moments The Mound appeared below them. She sank a little and floated in at the window of Diamond's room. There she laid him on his bed, covered him over, and in a moment he was sunk in a dreamless sleep.

CHAPTER TWENTY-SIX

# ONCE MORE

The next night Diamond was tired but eagerly waiting for the promised visit from North Wind. He fell asleep by his open window with his head on his hand and when he awoke he saw North Wind outside, holding by one hand to a top branch of the beech tree. Her hair and clothes went floating away behind her over the tree, whose top was swaying about while all the other trees were still.

"Are you ready, Diamond?" she asked.

"Yes," answered Diamond, "quite ready."

In a moment she was at the window, and her arms came in and took him. She sailed away so swiftly that at first he could see nothing but the clouds above and the earth below speeding past him. The night was warm, and in the lady's arms he did not feel the wind which down below was making waves in the ripe corn and ripples on the rivers and lakes. Finally they descended on the side of an open hill, just where a spring came bubbling out from beneath a stone.

"I am going to take you along this little brook," said North Wind. "I am not wanted for anything else tonight, so I can give you a treat."

She stooped over the stream and, holding Diamond down

close to the surface of it, glided along level with its flow as it ran down the hill. And the song of the brook came up into Diamond's ears, and grew and grew and changed with every turn. It seemed to Diamond to be singing the story of its life to him. And so it was. It began with a musical tinkle which changed to a babble and then to a gentle rushing. Sometimes its song would almost cease, and then break out again—tinkle, babble, and rush, all at once. At the bottom of the hill they came to a small river into which the brook flowed with a muffled but merry sound. Along the surface of the river they floated. Where it widened into a little lake, they would hover for a moment over a bed of water lilies or watch the fishes asleep among their roots below. Sometimes she would hold Diamond over a deep hollow of the river so he could look far into the cool stillness. Sometimes she would leave the river and sweep across a clover field. The bees were all at home and the clover was asleep. Then she would return and follow the river. It grew wider and wider as it went. Now the armies of wheat and oats would hang over its banks, and the willows would dip their low branches into its still waters. Wider and wider grew the stream until they came upon boats lying along its banks, rocking back and forth in the flutter of North Wind's garments. Then came houses on the banks, with lovely lawns and grand trees. And in parts the river was so high that some of the grass and the roots of some of the trees were under water. Then they would leave the river and float about and over the houses, one after another—beautiful houses, which, like fine trees, had taken centuries to grow. There was scarcely a light to be seen and not a movement to be heard: all the people lay fast asleep.

"What a lot of dreams they must be dreaming!" said Diamond.

"Yes," returned North Wind. "They surely can't all be untrue—can they?"

"I should think it depends a little on who dreams them," suggested Diamond.

"Yes," said North Wind. "The people who think lies, and do lies, are very likely to dream lies. But the people who love what is true will surely now and then dream true things. But then something depends on whether the dreams are home grown, or whether the seed of them is blown over somebody else's garden wall. Ah! there's someone awake in this house!"

They were floating past a window in which a light was burning. Diamond heard a moan and looked up anxiously into North Wind's face.

"It's a lady," said North Wind. "She can't sleep because of the pain."

"Couldn't you do something for her?" said Diamond.

"No, I can't. But you could."

"What could I do?"

"Sing a little song to her."

"She wouldn't hear me."

"I will take you in, and then she will hear you."

"But I wouldn't have any business in her room, would I?"

"You may trust me, Diamond. I shall take as good care of the lady as of you. The window is open. Come."

By a shaded lamp a lady was seated trying to read, but moaning every minute. North Wind floated behind her chair, set Diamond down, and told him to sing something. He was a little frightened, but he thought a while, and then sang:

The sun is gone down,
    And the moon's in the sky,
But the sun will come up,
    And the moon be laid by.

The flower is asleep
    But it is not dead;
When the morning shines,
    It will lift its head.

When winter comes,
    Will it die?—no, no;
It will only hide
    From the frost and the snow.

Sure is the summer,
    Sure is the sun;
The night and the winter
    Are shadows that run.

The lady never lifted her eyes from her book, or her head from her hand.

As soon as Diamond had finished, North Wind lifted him and carried him away.

"Didn't the lady hear me?" asked Diamond when they were once more floating down the river.

"Oh yes, she heard you," answered North Wind.

"Why didn't she look to see who it was?"

"She didn't know you were there."

"How could she hear me, then?"

"She heard you with her heart. She thought the words came out of the book she was reading. She will search all through it tomorrow and not be able to find them. She'll never forget the meaning, but she'll never be able to remember the words."

"Won't it puzzle her if she sees them in Mr. Raymond's book?"

"Yes, it will. She will never be able to understand it."

"Until she gets to the back of the north wind," suggested Diamond.

"Until she gets to the back of the north wind," agreed the lady.

"Oh!" cried Diamond. "I know where we are. Do let me go into the old garden, and into Mother's room, and Diamond's stall. I wonder if the hole is still at the back of my bed. I would like to stay here all the rest of the night!"

"You can stay here as long as you like," said North Wind as she sailed over the house with him and set him down on the lawn at the back.

Diamond ran about the lawn for a little while in the moonlight. He found it changed and did not like it. He ran into the stable. There were no horses at all. He ran upstairs. The rooms were empty. The only thing left that he cared about was the hole in the wall where his little bed had stood. He ran down the stair again and out on the lawn. He threw himself down and began to cry. It was all so dreary!

"I thought I liked the place so much," said Diamond. "I suppose it's only the people in it that make you like a place, and when they're gone, it's dead. Do take me home, North Wind."

"Have you had enough of your old home already?"

"Yes, more than enough. It isn't a home at all now."

"Everything, dreaming and all," said North Wind, "has got a soul in it or else it's nothing, even a house. When the soul is gone we don't care about it. Some of our thoughts are worth nothing because they've got no soul in them. The brain puts them into the mind, not the mind into the brain."

"But how can you know about that, North Wind? You haven't got a body."

"If I hadn't you wouldn't know anything about me. No creature can know another without the help of a body. But it isn't the time to talk about that. It's time for you to go home."

So saying, North Wind lifted Diamond and took him away.

## Chapter Twenty-Seven

# At the Back of the North Wind

I did not see Diamond for a week or so after this, and then he told me all of what I have now told you. I would have been astonished at his being able even to report such conversations as he said he had with North Wind had I not known already that some children have profound insight into supernatural matters. And Diamond was certainly such a one. He never troubled his head about what people thought of him. He never hinted at knowing more than others. The wisest things he said came out when he wanted someone to help him with some difficulty he was in. He was never offended with Nanny and Jim for calling him a silly. He supposed there was something in it, though he could not quite understand what. I suspect that the other name they gave him, *God's Baby,* helped him feel good about whatever he was called.

Happily for me, I was as much interested in spiritual things as Diamond himself, and therefore I enjoyed talking to him about his conversations with North Wind.

"Could it all be dreaming, do you think, sir?" he asked me anxiously.

"I dare not say, Diamond," I answered. "But at least there is one thing you may be sure of, that there is still a better love than that of the wonderful person you call North Wind. Even if she is a dream, the dream of such a beautiful creature could not come to you by chance."

"Yes, I know," returned Diamond. "I know."

Then he was silent, but seemed more thoughtful than satisfied. The next time I saw him he looked paler than usual. "Have you seen your friend again?" I asked him.

"Yes," he answered solemnly.

"Did she take you out with her?"

"No. She did not speak to me. I woke all at once, as I usually do when I am going to see her, and there she was against the door into the big room, sitting just as I saw her sit on her own doorstep, as white as snow, and her eyes as blue as the heart of an iceberg. She looked at me, but never moved or spoke."

"Weren't you afraid?" I asked.

"No. Why should I have been?" he answered. "I only felt a little cold."

"Did she stay long?"

"I don't know. I fell asleep again. I think I have been rather cold ever since, though," he added with a smile.

I did not quite like this, but I said nothing.

Four days after, I called at The Mound. The maid who opened the door looked very serious, but I suspected nothing. When I reached the drawing room, I saw that Mrs. Raymond had been crying.

"Haven't you heard?" she asked, seeing my questioning looks.

"I've heard nothing," I answered.

"This morning we found our dear little Diamond lying on the floor of the big attic room, just outside his own door—fast asleep, or so we thought. But when we picked him up, we did not think he was asleep. We saw that—"

Here the kindhearted lady broke out crying again.

"May I go and see him?" I asked.

"Yes," she sobbed. "You know your way up to the top of the tower."

I walked up the winding stair and entered his room. A lovely figure, as white as could be, was lying on the bed. I saw at once how it was. They thought he was dead.

I knew that he had gone to the back of the north wind.